Two Sighted

Even with her shaky past, Aislinn can't help but to secretly want Kyle. When she witnesses his death in a vision, how can she tell him without giving away her secret or her lust?

Aislinn Campbell is a clairvoyant, the latest in a long line of first-born daughters to the previous first-born daughter. All of them have fiery red hair and a second sight. Hiding from her ex in the presence of a sexy ex-military millionaire seems the safest way to start over. Until she "sees" his death.

Kyle Turner III has been keeping a close eye on Aislinn. There's nothing he doesn't know about his personal assistant, including her secret and ugly past. He also wants her in his bed more than his next breath. When he receives an anonymous warning that something might happen at his annual Fourth of July bash, he doesn't take it lightly. He knows exactly who sent the warning and he knows she's being watched by her bastard of an ex.

After he's injured in an accident, Kyle isn't about to leave Aislinn unprotected for a second. He coaxes her into more than just tending to his wounds. Because making Aislinn believe in him and her together far outweighs anything her ex can dish out.

Warning, this title contains the following: explicit sex, violence and graphic language.

The Strength of Three

Christina Marshall has no desire to have a man in her life. TJ McFee and Jonathan Winslow are on a mission to change her mind.

As the daughter of an abusive drunk, Christina could care less about the lack of men in her life. So why is she having seriously erotic dreams about two of her bosses?

Jon and TJ are men who go after what they want and right now their focus is on a certain blonde-haired, brown-eyed nymph who's done her best to blow off anyone of the XY persuasion. She's a challenge. Never let it be said that either one of them ignore a challenge.

Their seduction is set off course when Christina's mother dies and her father reinstates himself in her life. When accusations of murder fly, Chris must find a way to learn to trust both Jon and TJ. Her very life may depend on it.

Warning, this title contains the following: Blindfolds and bondage and sex—oh my. Ooh, and let's not forget about the m/f/m ménage and the graphic language.

Look for these titles by

Annmarie McKenna

Now Available:

Between a Ridge and a Hard Place

Blackmailed

Checkmate

Fantasmagorical (Sins of Summer)

Look What Santa Brought

Mystified

Seeing Eye Mate

Finding Strength

Annmarie McKenna

A Samhain Publishing, Ltd. publication.

Samhain Publishing, Ltd.
577 Mulberry Street, Suite 1520
Macon, GA 31201
www.samhainpublishing.com

Finding Strength
Print ISBN: 978-1-59998-805-4

Editing by Sasha Knight
Cover by Scott Carpenter

Two Sighted, 1-59998-476-8
First Samhain Publishing, Ltd. electronic publication: May 2007
The Strength of Three, 1-59998-553-5
First Samhain Publishing, Ltd. electronic publication: August 2007
First Samhain Publishing, Ltd. print publication: June 2008

Contents

Two Sighted

Dedication

Debbie Chisnell~Thanks for the help and the distractions. ☺

Chapter One

Bright light from the full moon glinted off the stainless-steel appliances in the immaculate kitchen. A scream echoed through the large space, drowning out the grunts and moans coming from the two men fighting near the center, arms locked in a combative embrace. The sickening thud of flesh on flesh was followed by a spurt of blood that showered the island countertop. The man dressed in black from head to toe took advantage, flinging them both to the ground with a bone-jarring crunch. He rolled, kneeling above the other man, who was wearing only boxers. With a snick, the man in black flicked open a switchblade. He swung it in an arc above his head, catching the moonlight, making the metal glow. The knife slashed through the air into the bare chest of the man below and another scream pierced the kitchen's confines.

"Yoo-hoo."

Aislinn Campbell sucked in a breath and shook her head, trying to ward off the last vestiges of the vision plaguing her yet again.

"Are you there, hon? Earth to Aislinn." Christina Marshall, the closest friend Aislinn had—the only friend she had—waved a hand in front of her face.

Aislinn had tried more times than she could count not to get close to the uber-bubbly personality that was Chris, to no avail. Chris had insinuated herself in Aislinn's life and never looked back.

Aislinn flushed with embarrassment. Of all the times for her to have a vision—at work in front of numerous coworkers. Great. She could probably count the minutes until word got around about her freakiness. Fighting the urge to cover her ears against the memories of past taunts, she fisted her hands on the arms of the ergonomic computer chair.

Her gaze traveled from one side of the room to the other, taking everything in. Mr. Turner liked the open work spaces instead of offices that shut everyone away. It was a fun atmosphere, which in turn led to lower turnover of employees and more production. No one seemed to be looking at her, not even Chris, who hopefully was too busy picking on her fingernail to notice Aislinn's distress.

"So how late did he make you stay last night?" Chris's focus remained on her nails but Aislinn heard the hint of amusement touching her voice.

Aislinn cleared her throat. "What?" Her friend wasn't acting like she'd noticed her momentary space out. Well, except for the *Earth to Aislinn* comment.

Chris dropped her hand and propped a butt cheek on the corner of Aislinn's desk. She looked her typical bored self, but Aislinn could see her attention was focused on something. Her gaze darted between the bank of elevators and Aislinn.

If she didn't know better, Aislinn might be offended. Despite Chris's protests, she was seriously interested in one of their boss's bodyguards. Aislinn hadn't figured out which one yet. And she didn't care. No man would ever have that kind of hold over her again.

"You know," Chris murmured. "Last night. The meeting. How long did he make you stay?"

"Oh. That. Not too late. Seven twenty-eight."

Chris laughed. "Not too late, but late enough you noticed the exact minute you walked out the door? Were his groupies with him?" she sneered.

Aislinn straightened the paperwork on her desk. Not even eight o'clock in the morning and already Mr. Turner had four messages. Her mouth went dry thinking about Kyle Turner III. Somehow she had to warn him without drawing attention to herself. She'd left him an email, but who knew if he'd even open it. Most of the time he left the menial task to her.

So she'd have to open her own email and then tell him what it said without letting on that she'd been the one to send it.

And just how would she go about that? *You got this strange email, Mr. Turner. It says, "Please watch yourself. I think someone's going to kill you in a kitchen."*

She could see it now. He'd look up at her from beneath his mile-long eyelashes with those gorgeous cornflower blue eyes, the corner of his mouth would quirk and he'd say, "Haven't I told you to stop opening strange emails? You're going to get our entire system infected with a virus."

Not to mention he would consider her for a "whacko of the century" award. She could imagine the padded cell with her name on it. Either that or his groupies, as Chris referred to them, would call her an accomplice to whatever nefarious demise was planned for Mr. Turner and have her locked away in a different kind of cell. One with bars, a disgusting toilet, a bunk with grungy, paper-thin mattresses and a cellmate named Large Marge.

Either way she wouldn't have to worry ever again about David. Her ex would have no access to her in jail. Huh. Maybe she should think on the possibility some more... Jail couldn't be all that bad. Food cooked for her, exercise time, TV time—good Lord! She was actually contemplating going to jail to get away from the man who should be there himself. What did that say about her?

Aislinn shook her head and forced herself to unclench the arms of the chair she'd taken hold of at some point for a second time.

"Man you are in another world today. What's up, chickie?" Chris crossed her arms over her chest.

"Nothing," Aislinn mumbled, rearranging her desk. Since when had she become OCD? "I've got a lot to do today and you're sitting on my faxes."

Chris lifted her butt and Aislinn yanked the papers out from under her.

"Were his groupies with him? Did they walk you to your car at least? Nothing about them seems at all civil. Do you think they ever leave Mr. Turner's side, or do you think the three of them sleep together too?" Chris had a habit of pulling questions out of thin air just for the sake of speaking. She was a chatterbox. The quirk was probably one of the reasons Aislinn liked the woman so much. Chris reminded Aislinn of her mother. Darla Campbell could talk the ears off anyone.

Aislinn snickered. "Yes, yes, and I have a feeling none of those men have ever been near a bed at the same time. Well, a real bed anyway. Probably when they were in the military they spent a lot of time watching each other's backs when they slept." She paused and cocked her head, thinking about something she'd seen a few weeks ago involving a blonde bombshell of a model and her friend's "groupies". "On second thought, TJ and Jonathan might be in cahoots." She winked at Chris. Talking about the two men was bound to raise Chris's hackles.

"No way."

Aislinn hid a smile at Chris's outright denial. "I was kidding," she consoled and watched Chris's shoulders droop. A second later her friend's back went ramrod straight.

"Speak of the devils." Chris jumped from her seat on the desk and straightened her clothes. The woman was practically primping herself. It wouldn't have surprised Aislinn if Chris ran her fingers through her hair too and dabbed on some lipstick.

Aislinn looked through the wall of glass at the three men making their way across the expansive lobby from the elevators. She fought the temptation to do some primping of her own. Her pulse sped up and her breath hitched the same way it did every time Kyle Turner III came near. Strange, considering she never wanted to be with a man again.

"Way too much testosterone right there if you ask me. Eighteen feet plus of packed muscle, tanned bods, gorgeous hair and enough charm to coax a snake to part from its skin. Throw in Jon's clear blue eyes and TJ's fathomless brown ones and what have you got? Sex on wheels," Chris grunted. "They practically swagger. Can you see them in long dusters and cowboy hats? Picture an old western film and them moving across a dusty street in slow motion. It's disgusting."

Aislinn snorted. "Is that why you're fixing yourself up?" Damn. The duster image was a nice one. She could see Kyle in one of those. And nothing else. *Oh God.*

"TJ will sleep with any woman who moves and Jonathan with anyone blonde and blue eyed. They both think they're God's gift and have egos the size of Texas." Chris's words wiped the vision from Aislinn's mind.

"For someone who says they can't stand TJ and Jonathan, you sure talk about them a lot. The color of their eyes, how sexy they are. Maybe you really want them." Aislinn stood and gathered up the message slips, a memo pad and a pencil. Kyle was a creature of habit and liked to have her attention first thing in the morning.

She shrugged off the feeling he asked her to join him for coffee for more than just catching up on what she'd done in the hour before he arrived.

Chris's mouth opened and closed and her cheeks turned red. "I do not," she hissed, keeping her voice low as they drew nearer.

"Uh-huh," Aislinn agreed, sarcastically.

"Morning, ladies," Kyle said, sauntering up to them like he owned the place.

Oh yeah. He did. Anybody who employed two bodyguards on a round the clock basis certainly owned the business.

"Good morning, Mr. Turner." Chris turned to Aislinn. "Lunch, Ais? Mexican?"

"Yes." Where else would they go? Their chicken tortilla soup was to die for.

"Can we come too?"

Aislinn nearly laughed at the pitiful puppy-dog-eyes expression on Jon's face.

Chris practically lifted her nose in the air. "No."

"Can you feel the love, Teej?"

"I can feel it, Jon." TJ put a hand over his heart in a wounded way.

"Stuff it, groupies. Later, Ais." Chris walked away, but not before Aislinn saw how red her ears were.

Totally unaffected by TJ and Jonathan. *And pigs could fly.* The woman talked about them nonstop until one or both appeared and then she clammed up and threw them a cold shoulder. Her attitude reminded Aislinn of a high-school crush where you really liked a boy but you didn't want him to know it so you were mean to him rather than telling him how you really felt. It was still a type of flirting in a roundabout way.

"Are you ready?" Kyle's deep voice rolled through her body, giving her goose bumps and the insane thought he was talking about more than work.

"Absolutely." Aislinn smiled and fought the temptation to lean into the warm hand he placed at the small of her back as he guided her to his office. She'd been there done that with David. Look what it had gotten her. A ton of bruises, a life in hiding and a lot of bottled-up secrets.

Aislinn looked fucking gorgeous this morning, as always. Freckles danced across her nose and cheeks. Kyle wanted to count them. With his lips. Her green eyes sparkled like brilliant emeralds from the laughter she'd been engaged in with Christina a minute ago. Sometime soon she'd laugh with him the same way. He was working on it, slowly but surely.

When she walked, the unruly red hair she had in its usual ponytail swished across the back of her neck, trickling over delicate skin. When he finally got her into bed, that space would be one of the first places he tasted. Aislinn never quite pulled the hair all the way through the band, but left the ends tucked in so the tail became a bun. Sort of, he guessed. Kyle had no clue what women called those particular things.

He only knew he couldn't wait to strip the elastic out of her hair and feel all those glorious fire red strands sliding over his thighs as she sucked his cock.

His dick twitched inside his jeans, coming to life the way it had every day for the last six months. If her past was anything to go by—and he knew it was—he had very little time left to make her his before she bolted again. He wasn't about to let that happen. It was time for her to stop running. And he was the man prepared to see to her safety.

She didn't know it, but Kyle had been keeping a periodic eye on her since the moment he'd learned the reason she'd come to Turner Industries in the first place. Hell, she'd only been there for three days when his private investigator had come in with a background check on Aislinn—a background that included an abusive ex who had stalked and tormented the fiery redhead until she felt the need to get a restraining order.

The order had only succeeded in pissing the bastard off to the point of attack. According to the police reports, Aislinn had barely lived through the terrifying ordeal. Kyle fisted his hands, remembering the pictures he'd seen of her battered face. The fucker should be in jail. Instead he was out there somewhere, hiding like the little mole he was.

Where the urge to protect her so fiercely came from, Kyle had no idea. He only knew that from the second she'd walked into his office, he had to have her. The background check had given him pause and made him back off when he would have started in immediately trying to make her his. If he waited much longer, his cock was likely to shrivel up and fall off from lack of use. It knew Kyle's hand in explicit detail, but it wanted the soft recesses it would find buried deep in Aislinn's pussy.

He fully applauded her attempt to flee David Tarkell. She'd done an excellent job, moving from place to place, never staying in one location for more than eight months or so, never getting attached to the people she worked with. Except she had this time. He could tell how close she'd gotten to Christina. He even recognized her initial wariness to do so.

"Coffee, Mr. Turner?"

He growled low in his throat, loud enough for her to hear, if the way her spine stiffened was any indication. Kyle hated the way she said his name. Or rather, didn't. No matter how many times he'd asked her to call him Kyle, she still refused. He guessed it was some sort of defense mechanism. If she didn't get close to anyone, it was easier to move on.

"Coffee?"

Kyle cleared his throat. "Please."

She moved past him, carefully skirting his body even as he crowded her between himself and the desk. Her sharp, white teeth bit on the full lower lip he couldn't wait to taste.

He inhaled her scent as she came within inches of him—a combination of something fruity from whatever shampoo she washed her hair with and all woman. Based on the fact he could smell her sweet essence, she sure as hell wasn't as immune to him as she would like to believe. He would bet anything she was wet under the shapeless black slacks.

He snorted. If she thought she was hiding anything from him, she was sadly mistaken. She could wear a potato sack and he'd still be able to see her great body. The only thing left to do was strip the material from her so he could actually feel the perfect skin he knew he would find beneath.

"Do you have a duster?" she blurted, rolling the words together.

Kyle jerked his gaze from her ass to her face as she turned around, coffee in one shaky hand, eyes wide, lip still being worried by those teeth.

Fuck. At the rate she was going, she'd have a hole in that lip by noon. He moved to her slowly, an eyebrow quirked. She'd thrown him for a loop for sure.

"As in...feather?" he asked, getting closer and not even beginning to imagine where she was headed with the question. He knew what he'd like to do with a feather duster and a whole lot of her gorgeous, bare skin.

She swallowed and two spots of red graced her pale cheeks.

"Oh God." Her cheeks got impossibly redder and he bit back a smile.

"And just why is it you want to know if I have a feather duster?" he whispered, running his knuckles up the arm holding out the mug. Beneath the white blouse she wore, her nipples puckered. He wondered if she even noticed how her body responded to him because he sure the hell did. She tensed and sucked in a breath, but he didn't let up. It was time for her to stop running.

Aislinn cringed and croaked, "Not feather." She stepped back, out of reach, but the counter stopped her and he moved in again.

"No?"

She shook her head vigorously enough to slosh hot coffee over the rim and onto her delicate skin.

"Shit." Kyle jerked the mug from her hand as she squeaked in pain, and he turned her to face the sink.

He plunked the coffee down, ignoring the spill of more dark liquid, and flipped on the faucet. Grabbing her wrist, Kyle guided her hand under the cold water and held it there. His heart thumped against her upper back right between her shoulder blades as he held her snugly against his chest. Her bottom cradled his erection and he bit back a curse. The damn thing should have gone bye-bye the second he'd seen her injured, instead it grew bigger at her nearness.

She hissed at the cool against the burn and Kyle rubbed his thumb over the pink area just above her thumb. It wouldn't even blister, he didn't think. He pulled her hand from the stream and looked closer at the damage. What he saw made his temper explode.

"What the fuck is this, Aislinn?"

She gasped and yanked her hand from his hold, burying it behind the other at her belly.

Kyle jerked her around to face him, cursing under his breath when he saw the panicked look. He eased her hands apart and recaptured the injured one to inspect it again.

Why the fuck hadn't he seen the fading white scars gracing her hand before? Because he hadn't been looking at her hands, that's why.

Rage flared to life. If he ever caught the motherfucker who'd done this to her, he'd kill the bastard himself. And since he knew exactly who'd done it, he was one step away from murder.

"It's nothing," she cried and tried to pull away.

This time, Kyle held fast. "Bullshit," he spat and turned her hand over. The healed scars covered her palm too. In his book they were clearly defensive wounds. He smoothed over all of them and fought the desire to punch something for the injustice done to her.

"Who did it?" he rasped, knowing full well who the culprit was. If Aislinn had any chance of getting over David Tarkell she would have to talk to someone.

"No one," she insisted, tugging harder.

Kyle whipped his gaze to her startled one. "You did this to yourself?" He didn't believe it for a second but Jesus, he'd heard of people who hurt themselves when they felt they had no other outlet. Cutters, he thought they were called. He closed his eyes against the pain threatening to seize him. Please God, don't let her be that far gone.

"No, I..."

He opened his eyes and met hers again. They were wild, searching everywhere but him.

"You what?" he demanded.

He had to give her credit. She straightened her spine and lifted her chin. "*I* didn't do it." This time she twisted her hand in his and pulled free. He let her, allowing her the space she needed.

"Then who did?" He might have let go but no way was he backing down.

"My ex, all right!"

Finally. He refrained from pumping his fist in the air. This was the first time she'd ever mentioned him. Instead he crossed his arms over his chest.

He stared hard at her. "He can't hurt you anymore, you know that, don't you?"

Chapter Two

Aislinn sucked in a breath and felt the blood drain from her face, leaving her dizzy. "What are you talking about?"

Kyle sighed and dropped his arms.

What the hell was going on here? She'd gone from getting her boss coffee and wondering how to tell the six–foot-three, muscle-packed, ex-Special Forces, blond stud his life was in danger to having her own sordid life thrown out before her. She didn't want to do this. Not with him. Not with anyone. She glanced at the door, judging the distance of her getaway and fighting the flight instinct at the same time.

"What am I talking about?" he snarled. "The fact that you've been here for six months and have never said one word about yourself. The fact that you have defensive wounds on your hand which clearly say you've either been attacked or cut yourself, which I highly doubt. The fact that I know everything there is to know about you and I know you're safe here with me and the fact that I want to fuck you so bad I can taste it. That's what I'm talking about."

Stunned, Aislinn leaned on the counter for support and tried to breathe. He wanted to fuck her? It was almost laughable. According to David, she was frigid. Based on the way her body reacted to the sound of Kyle's voice, she was beginning to wonder if David had been wrong. Still, if Kyle had any clue she'd never once had an orgasm he'd probably turn tail and run. How many men would bother with a woman who couldn't perform in bed?

Yet, at the moment, her nipples were rubbing against her bra, making her want to smooth the ache away with her palms, and her tummy was doing a dance. She ought to be used to her response to his nearness by now.

Then the other half of what he'd said filtered through. How much did he know, and how? She'd never said a word, just like he mentioned. Her knees wobbled and she started to sink to the ground.

"Damn it," came the hiss from above her.

Black dots swam in her vision. Strong arms lifted her and cradled her against a hard chest. Aislinn buried her nose there. Shame riddled her.

"Did you eat this morning?" Kyle demanded, lowering her to the long sofa on the far wall.

She nodded and gripped his shirt in her hands, unwilling to let go, but knowing she should. Had to. She didn't want his pity. His hands covered hers and pried them from the silky fabric, then transferred them both into one of his. Big, warm, calloused fingers enveloped hers. He knelt in front of her and lifted her chin with his thumb.

"Nothing will happen to you here," he assured her, his tone brooking no argument. "I know everything."

Aislinn sucked in her bottom lip and bit down on it.

"Christ, woman, if you don't stop biting that lip, I'm going to turn you over my knee and spank you." He tugged the offended lip from beneath her teeth and caressed it with a fingertip.

Her heart pounded like it wanted to leap from her chest

and her breath caught in her throat. It took precious seconds for her to decide if he'd really just threatened to spank her or if she'd imagined it in some depraved corner of her mind. The way he said spank brought to mind nothing but intense pleasure, not pain.

She didn't think Kyle was anything like David but her track record proved she knew nothing about men. David had been nice once too.

Kyle angled closer. Instead of pulling away, she found herself meeting him halfway. Everything else slipped from her brain. Everything except his mouth, which crept dangerously close to her own. Her eyes slid shut and she breathed in his scent. She wanted this. For the first time in her adult life, she wanted a man to kiss her. Wanted Kyle to kiss her. No one else. She wanted Kyle to see her as a desirable woman, not one with an ugly past.

"Yes, spank. You heard me right, Aislinn." His breath puffed out on her lips.

And then he was there, his mouth on hers, his tongue demanding entrance, which she gave him way too easily.

She opened and fumbled her tongue on his, feeling like a virgin kissing for the first time. He tasted minty like he'd just brushed his teeth. There was nothing virgin on Kyle's end though. He expertly insinuated himself in her mouth, feasting on her, tilting her head for better access. Aislinn leaned into him, wanting more, needing more. She couldn't get close enough. It was a position she'd never found herself in.

Threading a hand in the hair at her nape, Kyle pulled back and looked at her. "Slow down, baby. We've got all the time in the world for this."

The spell broke with a whoosh. Memories flooded, overriding her desire and bringing back all the pain and insecurities. She wasn't good enough. She never would be. David had made that clear as day. And *she* would never let a man have control over her again.

Aislinn scrambled off the couch, thankful when Kyle let her get up. She twisted her hands in front of her. Her belly turned over when she looked at Kyle and saw the dismay on his face. He seemed almost hurt.

But he had broken the kiss, not her. Why should he feel pain?

"Hey," he said, standing and then stalking toward her again. "I know what you're thinking, Aislinn." He traced the eyebrow above her right eye with a gentle finger. "We aren't over by a long shot, sweetheart. I just don't want it to happen here, in my office. On a couch." Kyle eased her against his body, enfolding her in a semi-loose embrace, one she could easily escape. For that she was grateful. His breath feathered her ear, making her shiver.

"When I get in you the first time, we'll be in a bed. And you will be more than ready for me. Drenching wet." He kissed the shell of her ear and down her neck. "There will be no inch of your body I haven't tasted." His mouth moved to the V at the base of her throat and up the other side.

Aislinn moaned and tilted her head. He made her forget who she really was, casting a spell over her with his kisses alone. Her skin tingled in anticipation. A tiny flicker of something she'd never experienced before pulsed between her legs, making her fidget and want to rub herself against the hardness pressing into her belly. The feeling was entirely alien, and yet felt so good. Could she do this?

No. No. She couldn't let herself be drawn into his world. She wouldn't lose herself to another man. Ever.

So why couldn't she make herself pull away from him now?

"No, wait. Me licking every delectable inch of you will have to wait 'til round two." Kyle trailed his fingers down the length of her arms and she let him. Let him make her feel like a goddess when she knew giving in to him would only lead to trouble. And pain and heartache. It was time to leave. She needed to get away from him before this went one step further. Why couldn't she make her feet move?

"The first time will be fast and furious," he mumbled, teasing her mouth open again and thrusting his tongue home.

Both of his hands lifted to tangle in her ponytail, pulling it loose from its semi-bun. Their bodies were plastered together. She felt his penis against her belly. Oh God, it was so big.

Aislinn knew firsthand what kind of weapon it would make, had felt the pain David had inflicted on her vagina, her mouth and her bottom, and the searing humiliation she had to live with afterward.

She panicked and threw her hands between them, pushing for all she was worth. With a desperate cry she tore free. Kyle shoved a hand through his hair, leaving it disheveled and sexier than ever.

Aislinn swallowed and looked away, hating what had become of her life. Afraid of sex and men. Afraid of getting close to anyone again. She'd have to apologize to Kyle. Another lesson à la David. Always apologize for pissing him off before he brought the wrath of God down on her.

Tears sprang to her eyes. Damn. She thought she'd gotten over this. Thought she'd finally become a stronger woman. She had, in some respects, but apparently not when it came to men. No matter how much she wanted the one standing in front of her, going any further would be a disaster.

Readying herself for whatever blow might land, she faced him. "I'm sorry, Mr. Turner." Her chin wobbled despite her attempt to remain strong.

Kyle smashed his face behind his hands and refrained from yelling in frustration and scaring her off. What had he thought would happen? That he'd kiss her and she'd be cured? Thank God he'd at least gotten the preliminaries out of the way. As long as he could make her see and understand that he could protect her, and that she was safer staying here than running again, he'd have the time he needed to change her mind about him.

He lowered his hands. Tears welled in her eyes, one spilling over her lower lashes and tracking down her cheek. One single tear and his stomach felt weighed down with lead, deflating his raging hard-on in half a second.

He stayed where he was. No need to cause her further distress. That was the last thing he wanted.

"What are you sorry about, baby?"

Her gaze jerked to his, another tear dropping off, and her mouth opened and closed.

"You...I...I didn't mean to lead you on."

Kyle shut his eyes and counted to ten. Then twenty. Hell, fifty wouldn't have been enough.

"Jesus, baby." Kyle wanted to shout, but if he saw her flinch it would make him come unglued. "Lead me on?" he rasped. "If anyone's sorry, it's me. I shouldn't have forced you."

She wrung her hands.

"David really did a number on you, didn't he, baby?"

"How did you know his name?" she whispered.

"I told you, I know everything."

"How?" She looked ready to faint.

"Aislinn, sit down before you fall down."

She did. Or rather, she perched on the very edge of the couch, prepared to bolt if need be. He watched her eye the distance to the door yet again and was getting damned tired of her constant visual assessment of escape routes. He didn't blame her one bit after what she'd been through, he just wanted her to feel safe enough in his presence that she wouldn't have the need to size up her location. Of course he knew all about keeping one's back to the wall.

"Would it help if I opened it?"

"What?" She jerked her gaze back to him.

"The door. Would it make you more comfortable if I opened the door?"

Indecision marred her pretty features. She schooled them and straightened. Kyle released the breath he'd been holding.

"No." She shook her head.

"Good." He didn't want an audience.

"How do you know about David?" she asked again, strength returning to her voice.

"I'm not going to lie to you, Aislinn."

"I didn't ask you to, Kyle."

His heart stopped hearing his name roll off her lips. "Say it again."

"I didn't ask—"

"Not that."

She tilted her head in confusion.

"My name, Aislinn. Say my name again."

For a long moment she paused, pursing her lips. She hadn't meant to say it apparently, which meant he was making headway of a sort. If she said his name unconsciously, in the heat of battle, it meant she wasn't as immune to him as she'd like to be. Her kisses said the same thing.

"Kyle," she muttered.

He smiled. "Again."

"Why?" she demanded with a huff.

"Because I've waited six long, fucking months to hear it and now that you've said it once, you can't go back."

"I can."

The indignancy in her words made him chuckle and he bent over her, rubbing his nose on hers and invading her space another time. It was a risky move but she needed to get used to being near him. He planned on spending a lot of time close enough to touch her.

"You can't, Aislinn. Get it through your pretty little head. You and I will make love, and you will scream my name when you come. Over and over and over. As many times as I want to make you come."

Kyle stood before she could protest and walked to his desk chair. He sat and reached for a file folder. When he glanced back at her she looked disappointed.

"I can't," she said with a semi-hysterical laugh and slapped her thighs.

"You can't what?"

Her chin rose. "I can't come."

He snorted. "Every woman can come." With the proper lover, anyway. There were probably a few who were physically incapable but Kyle had yet to meet any of them.

"Not me."

Kyle held his pencil so tightly he felt the wood crack in his palm. "Sweetheart, just because your bastard ex never gave you the chance, doesn't mean you can't."

Her chest rose on a deep inhalation and her lips parted. Hell, even from the distance separating her from him he saw her pupils dilate.

"Did I have any messages?" he asked, neatly avoiding the topic of her prick ex and the fact he'd never given her pleasure.

He hid his smile—his teeth were starting to hurt from gritting them so much—at her flustered look and watched her compose herself.

"Yes," she said, reaching for the slips of pink paper she'd brought in with her.

"Go ahead."

"No."

Kyle barked out in laughter. Aislinn jumped. He sat back in his seat and twisted it from side to side. "Six months we've been doing this every morning. Six months and you've never once told me no. Why today?"

Bastard. He knew why. She'd like to wipe the cocky smile right off his face. Where was it written that a man could get a woman all hot and bothered—when they didn't want to be, no less—and then turn all business in a second flat?

She could practically feel her blood boiling beneath her skin. Her entire body was probably the same hot pink as her cheeks.

"Today, because you've never said before you were having me watched." There. Let him wonder if maybe he hadn't done a good job trying to get her all worked up.

Her boss raised an eyebrow. "I don't remember saying I was having you watched."

Well, he had her there, didn't he? She searched her brain but found he was right. He hadn't actually said anything about watching her. But he knew about David and how else would he know those things unless... Lord, why had she ever said anything about the damn duster?

If she had just kept her mouth shut, they would have gone through their normal morning routine. There would never have been a stray of topics and Aislinn would be sitting out at her desk right now—sipping coffee, filing reports, filling out forms and working on how to keep her boss out of kitchens. But no. Christina had put the rogue image of Kyle, naked behind a duster, in her head. She groaned inwardly.

"I'm a smart woman, Mr. Tur—"

"Hey," he snapped. "You won't get away with it, Aislinn."

She gritted her teeth. "Kyle, then," she ground out. "You may not have said anything about following me, but—"

"Now I'm following you?"

"You are an infuriating man."

He grinned. She should have been irritated to hell by the action. She wanted to be. Instead it only melted something inside her heart. Kyle made it nearly impossible for her to stay mad at him. A miracle in itself since she hated all men.

Liar.

She took a deep breath. "How did you know about David?"

Kyle shrugged. "I do background checks on all my employees, particularly the ones who will be working the closest to me. I had to do a lot of digging for yours. To quote you, I'm a smart man."

She was floored. "But...why did you hire me if you knew about me?"

He snorted. "You have to ask me that after the speech I just gave you?"

Aislinn swallowed. She hadn't gotten up this morning with

anything on her mind other than warning her boss of imminent danger. Now she found herself embroiled in digging up a past she wished dead and picturing the man sitting across from her naked. Ripped abs, sleek tanned skin, a thick cock jutting out in anticipation. Of her. Cheeks flaring, she licked her lips and tried to shake the image.

"You're thinking about it, aren't you?"

"No," she hissed, hating being caught in a lie.

"You are."

"You have four messages." She bit her tongue and handed the slips to him, careful not to touch any part of his fingers. "The caterer's confirming, Michael Whitehall wanting to know why his wife hasn't been caught yet, Mrs. Givens can't find Fluffy again and Crystal called. Again. She sounds...sweet," she couldn't help adding.

"You don't approve of Crystal?"

Aislinn cleared her throat and smoothed an invisible wrinkle on her shirt. She'd never questioned his business before. Her flustered attitude was all his fault.

"I don't know Crystal," she murmured, trying to redeem herself. She wished now she had begged him to open the door instead of trying to be a tough girl. She looked anywhere but at him and prayed he was done with her for the day.

His silence got to her. She lifted her gaze to find him smiling at her. Again. Her body melted. Impossible. Frigid women did not melt in front of smiling egotistical men, nor did their nipples tighten or their wombs clench. Sweat popped out on her forehead. She had to get out of here.

"Anyway," she said, standing, "you also have several emails to look at." She edged toward the door and freedom, for at least the next few minutes. "Some of them looked important, so make sure you actually *read* them."

"You mean you're not going to tell me what's in them today?"

"No."

"I'm impressed." Kyle crossed his arms over his chest. "That makes three noes this morning."

She reached for the handle, praying he wouldn't say something stupid like, "Come back here and tell me what's so damned important in these emails you want to make sure *I* read them this morning."

"Wait just a minute," Kyle's voice rumbled. "I want to know what's in these emails that is making you not want to read them today."

Damn it. She'd been so close to escape. Aislinn wiped a sticky palm on her hip and licked her lips, moistening the suddenly dry skin. "Nothing, I've just got quite a bit to do, you know, with last-minute details of the party and such and, like you said, you're a smart man."

If the man smiled one more time at her she was going to scream.

"By all means, work on the party. I will see you there, right?"

She knew it wasn't a request. All of the employees went to his annual Fourth of July party. Why wouldn't they? Held on his multi-acreage-wide lakefront property, there was food, dancing, a bonfire and a massive fireworks display, from everything Chris had told her. Plus, Kyle handed out half-year bonuses. The man was generous to a fault.

Aislinn nodded once. Of course she would be there. If she didn't show up, he'd more than likely sic TJ and Jon on her and have them drag her there anyway.

She slipped out the door, his laughter ringing out behind

her. Hell yes, she was running. She needed to put some space between them. *Please, God, let him read those emails.* She did not relish the idea of telling him face-to-face and revealing more of herself than he already knew, which seemed to be a whole lot more than anyone else.

For a second she pondered leaving. The urge to get in her car, drive to her apartment and pack her bags was strong, but what he'd said was true. She most likely was safer here than anywhere else. With his and TJ's and Jonathan's backgrounds in the Special Forces who better to provide protection? Not to mention the type of business they ran. Spy equipment and high-tech gadgets used in finding people. It was one of the reasons she'd come to Turner Industries in the first place. She couldn't find a better business to hide in.

She'd been naïve in thinking he wouldn't use those same gadgets on her. Six months did seem a rather long time not to hear from her ex. Had she gotten lax or did she feel that much more comfortable in Kyle's presence?

As evidenced today, her body sure as hell wanted him. Was she ready for another stab at a relationship? Kyle might actually be a perfect candidate because he was a no-strings-attached kind of man with all his women. And it was more than clear he wanted her.

What could it hurt? Her pride, for one, when she didn't perform the way he thought she would. Good thing David had stripped most of hers away, she guessed. Not much more to get trampled.

Aislinn realized she'd been standing at her desk staring into space and slid into her seat. Straightening papers that didn't need straightening, she thought about what it might be like to make love to Kyle Turner III. What he'd said to her had certainly made her pussy weep for the first time. Ever.

Maybe enough time had passed. Maybe David really was history. Maybe he'd found another poor soul to pick on, God help her.

Determined to start moving on with her life without constantly looking over her shoulder, Aislinn resolved to...keep an open mind about Kyle. Yeah, she decided. If he ever kissed her again, she wouldn't try to keep herself from kissing him back.

ઉ઼

A couple of hours later, Kyle stared at his computer screen. Subtle was not Aislinn's middle name. Of course, if he hadn't already known about her clairvoyant ability, he might have handled this particular email a little differently. Like laugh and delete it.

One of his SEAL buddies had had a similar trait. Perhaps not as defined as Aislinn's gift of "seeing" the future, but he knew things intuitively. Things that had more than once saved the team's backside. Things that had gotten them out of various tight spots. You can bet your sweet ass he believed in what Aislinn could "see".

He idly rubbed his right thumb along his forefinger as he decided what to do with the information in front of him.

No kitchens. He could handle that. One of the reasons he employed a chef at home was because he couldn't boil water. Give him an MRE any day. At least he was used to the Meals Ready to Eat. Some of them were even palatable.

Question was, would he heed the warning? Maybe it was better to face his potential murderer head on, since he had no doubt Aislinn's prediction would come true. Running wasn't an option. He knew about it ahead of time and had an opportunity to change the way things panned out.

He hadn't told her the complete story. Not only did he know everything there was to know about her, but he'd also been in touch with her mother several times. He'd updated the woman whose daughter had been forced into hiding, letting her know Aislinn was safe from the bastard. Darla Campbell had been the one to tell him of Aislinn's ability—a talent the two women shared along with previous generations of females in the family.

Kyle admitted he was a little disappointed Aislinn hadn't told him about her gifts, but he understood. Why would she? In her mind, her clairvoyance only caused people to wonder if she was crazy. More than anything, it drew attention. And attention was the last thing she wanted right now. In fact, Kyle applauded her adeptness at keeping her secret.

A few times, from his office, he seen her off in another world, but she seemed more than capable of snapping out of it in time to prevent questions. Usually. Twice Kyle had stepped in and diverted a possible disaster. Both times she'd been sitting at her desk, a faraway look on her face, when someone had stopped to speak with her.

Kyle had simply walked out of his office and detoured them.

Thank God it didn't happen on a routine basis. If it did, he'd have made a space for her inside his office, something he knew she would protest.

He heard Aislinn's voice outside his door so he stood and stretched. Staring at the anonymous email wouldn't get him any closer to the answer.

Aislinn was grabbing her purse and gabbing with Christina when he stepped out the door.

"Where are you going?"

She gasped—he loved when she made those noises—and swung around. A mutinous look crossed her face. "To lunch."

"Yeah? Who with?" Not that he had any real right to ask.

"Chris."

"Ah." He nodded. "Where are you going?"

"You already asked that."

"I did. You told me lunch. Maybe I want to go to lunch. Where are you—"

"You can't." Christina's eyes widened in mortification.

Kyle turned to her, crossed his arms over his chest and leaned against the doorframe.

"How come? You gonna talk about the boss?" Why else would she look so panicked about going to lunch with him if they weren't going to discuss him?

Christina gulped and Aislinn smiled behind her hand. What the hell was going on?

He watched Christina's face as she did some quick thinking.

"Because, well, you usually go with your gr— I mean, TJ and Jonathan and you know what they say," Christina finally came up with.

"No," he said, trying not to chuckle at the poor woman he knew had a crush on one of his buddies. He wondered if she was aware they were attached at the hip and liked to share their women, or if she had any idea they'd set their sights on her. "Who are they, and what is it they say?"

"Oh, um." She waved her arm in the air, twisting her wrist around in circles. "Two's company...er, five's a crowd."

"Five?"

"Uh-huh." She looked at Aislinn for relief.

Aislinn took her time getting herself together. He bet Aislinn knew about Christina's crush too.

"Besides," she continued, "we have some girlie issues to discuss and I doubt you'd be comfortable talking about...tampons."

Kyle laughed. He couldn't hold it in any longer. "You're going to lunch to talk about the absorbency of feminine products?"

"Chris," Aislinn hissed and grabbed her elbow, pulling her toward the elevators. "Damn, woman. Talk about sticking your foot in your mouth. Couldn't you think of any other topic?"

"Have dinner with me tonight," Kyle called before they could get too far. He hated watching Aislinn's retreating back. The only time he wanted to see her back was when she was on her hands and knees in front of him, his cock buried deep inside her.

The girls spun around so quickly they bumped into each other.

Christina's chin lifted. "Excuse me?"

Aislinn shook her head in a firm no. Her lips formed a "shush", and her eyes narrowed. He smiled and stepped away from his perch.

"Yes," he said.

"No way," Christina retorted as if he were speaking to both of them.

Kyle ignored Christina's refusal and never took his gaze off Aislinn. He *would* win this round. "Have dinner with me," he repeated, standing toe-to-toe with her. Her mouth opened but nothing came out.

"I can't," Aislinn finally said.

He tilted his head and studied her. Weariness marked every

millimeter of her face.

"Why?"

"Because. I don't think it's proper to date employees."

"I'm not an employee," Kyle clarified. "Christina, why do you think Aislinn asked me about dusters earlier today?" he asked, still not looking away from Aislinn's eyes. There had to be a reason why she would suddenly ask him about something personal, and he had no doubt her closest friend Christina had put the idea in her head. Since he hadn't gotten the answer from Aislinn earlier maybe he could get it out of Christina.

Christina gasped and turned to Aislinn. "You didn't."

Bingo.

Aislinn's eyes narrowed into thin, angry lines.

"She did. Something about feather dusters."

"I did not," Aislinn yelled then slapped a hand over her mouth.

Kyle smiled. What had she and Chris been talking about this morning? His cock hardened thinking about the possibility they had been talking about him.

"Aislinn." There was a twinkle in Christina's eye as she admonished her friend with a new playful side Kyle could honestly say he hadn't seen before. She was more outgoing with the women at Turner but she gave men the cold shoulder. He'd leave the mystery to TJ and Jon to penetrate. No pun intended. "I never said feather, honey."

"I didn't either," Aislinn muttered, turning back to the elevators and grabbing Christina's arm again.

Christina glanced back over her shoulder. "I told her you and your groupies looked like cowboys wearing dusters walking through the old west."

The forwardness of her response shocked him. Groupies?

What the hell was that all about? He'd dig into all of it later, he decided, when he realized his date for the night was swaying those fine hips of hers farther and farther away.

"Dinner, Aislinn. Don't make me go home to a lonely kitchen to fend for myself." He issued his ultimatum with a soft command knowing she wouldn't be able to resist.

She choked and twisted in horror.

He had her.

Chapter Three

Kneeling, Aislinn threw the last piece of clothes from the dresser in her closet over her shoulder and groaned in defeat. Nothing. Absolutely nothing to wear for dinner with the boss. Kyle. The boss.

She dropped her head back and sighed.

God, she was going on a date. With her boss. Why? Why was she about to put herself in a situation with a man again?

She had the sudden urge to call her mom. Tears filled her vision and dripped down her cheeks. She swiped them away with an angry hand and sniffed. Damn it. The asshole was still controlling her life after all this time.

How long had it been since she'd talked to her own mother? How long since she'd heard her mom's sing-song voice telling her to listen to her dreams or to follow her heart?

Too long to remember. But the total cut from her previous life had been what was recommended to her by a man who knew how to make people disappear. She hadn't been able to part with her name in the end. A switch of names had made the situation seem too permanent, like she'd never be able to return home, so she'd chosen to live the life of a nomad, instead. Every eight months or so, she picked up and left.

In the beginning she'd moved every couple of months just trying to stay ahead of the demonic bastard who claimed to love her so much. He hadn't loved her at all. David had wanted to own her.

Aislinn sat back and drew her knees up to hug them. Maybe it was time to stand and face the music. Insinuate herself back into her old life. Show David what she'd become in her years of self-imposed exile.

What had she become? Was she a different person than the one who'd gone on the run?

The doorbell rang, startling her out of her musings.

"Shiiiit." She jumped to her feet and stared at the disaster surrounding her. Every article of clothing she owned lay strewn on the floor.

Thank God he wouldn't be in her bedroom.

At least, she didn't think he would. She couldn't really put anything past Kyle.

She hurried through her tiny rented house, still dressed in what she'd worn to work. That ought to make a good impression.

The doorbell pealed again.

She couldn't help but smile. "Impatient man. I'm coming."

Flipping open the curtain, Aislinn peeked out. And got a view full of flowers. A lot of flowers in a riot of colors. She twisted the deadbolt open and flung the door wide. "I can't believe you did this."

He lowered the flowers and Aislinn sucked in a breath at the angry slash of his eyebrows. "You didn't even ask who was standing out here, Aislinn."

Her heart stopped. Had she been wrong about him? She lifted her chin and steeled herself. "You invited me to dinner, said you'd be here at seven." She glanced at her watch. "It's six fifty-eight. And I looked out the window and only saw flowers. I knew this wasn't a good idea."

She tried to slam the door shut but Kyle stuck his big booted foot in the way. With little effort he pushed it open and stepped inside, crowding her back into the wall.

"I had the flowers up so I could make sure you were taking the proper precautions when answering the door." He pressed against her, smashing the bouquet between them.

She licked her lips. "I'm not stupid, Kyle."

"I know you're not, sweetheart, I just need to know nothing will happen to you when I'm not around," he said, softening his tone.

"I've been fine on my own all this time."

"There's no reason for you to be alone anymore."

"That's a little presumptuous, don't you think?"

His head lowered closer to her face. "Nope." His lips descended and meshed with hers.

Lava flowed through her veins, despite her anger at being yelled at like a five-year-old. Velvet softness swept around her mouth, minty and tangy, and she wanted to devour him. Her breath mingled with his. His hands cradled her face. It took a few seconds to realize the flowers were no longer between them.

Aislinn lifted her hands to his chest, unable to keep from touching him or exploring him with tentative fingers. He tilted her head and delved deeper into her mouth, sweeping into her and practically feasting on her.

Having never been kissed with such passion, she reciprocated, moaning and feeling like she wasn't getting enough.

She shifted her hips wanting to get closer, to ease an ache that started somewhere in her belly and trailed down between her legs.

His lips left hers and traveled along her chin, down her neck to the collar of her blouse. She whimpered and had the insane urge to rip the fabric wide open so he had better access to the points of her breasts tingling against her bra.

God where was this coming from? These riotous, foreign explosions of sensation.

Kyle spun them, his mouth still kissing over every inch of her skin, his hands roaming her back and down to her hips. His feet moved, pushing them further into the room. They paused for a moment and somewhere in her mind, Aislinn heard the door slam.

His lips returned to tease hers, his tongue licked and pressed between her teeth. They dueled in her mouth and shyly, Aislinn thrust into his.

Her knees hit the couch a second before she was spun wildly around again, and she fell into his lap with a squeal. Kyle cut her off, kissing her into oblivion, his groans meeting hers head on. Never breaking their kiss, he shifted her, bringing her legs across his, seating her bottom comfortably in his lap. Her hip ground into his erection and she panicked until his hand came up to cover her breast. Aislinn sank into him.

Exquisite. His thumb flicked over her nipple, his lips moved to her ear. Teeth nibbled on the soft flesh there and his breath tickled.

"Okay?"

Oh, God. She could weep. David had never asked her, just taken. She nodded once when what she really wanted was to beg.

"Feel, sweetheart, just feel," he whispered.

Feel? She was about to implode from the feelings. His hand wandered down her rib cage until she felt his rough fingertips against her bare skin. Her tummy muscles quivered in reaction.

She wanted...what? More? To stop? What?

He burrowed under her shirt and then the cotton of her bra to cup her breast. A light pinch on the already sensitive nipple shot lightning bolts through her. Her womb clenched and her clit ached. Aislinn squeezed her legs together and fought the temptation to rub the nubbin. Whatever was coming excited her like nothing else ever had.

She pulled away, breathing heavily. Everything in his face seemed sincere. But what if she didn't please him? Was now the time to show her gratitude? Why did part of her want to get on her knees and reciprocate? Would it make him angry for her to want to do that? God she was so confused. A jumble of emotions coursed through her. He made this seem so natural, so beautiful. What did he expect from her in return? Why hadn't he already demanded what he wanted?

"Come back here, Aislinn. I'm not finished with you yet," he murmured.

"Should I...touch—"

"No," he growled, yanking her back to his chest. "You touch me now and we'll never make it to dinner."

He pinched her nipple again and she arched into his callus-roughened fingertips.

She wanted to explore, but held back, unsure of how he'd react. David hadn't ever allowed her to touch him except when and where he wanted her to. Were all men the same?

Kyle pulled her close and resumed their kiss. Lord he made her forget everything. She could no longer help herself. She wanted to touch him so badly.

Before she could, his hand wandered south, pressing along her stomach, and he let his finger dip into her navel. She laughed into his mouth and felt his smile.

"Ticklish?"

"Guess so."

He fumbled at the button of her slacks. Aislinn held her breath and closed her eyes. Do or die time. If she couldn't come, he'd know the truth and she could leave. Get on with her life by putting aside men for the rest of it.

Long fingers pushed through the curls shielding her entrance.

"Breathe, sweetheart."

Oh, God, she wasn't. In fact, she was rigid against him, her fists gripping his shirt.

She took a conscious breath, filling her lungs, and let it out slowly. A fingertip grazed over her clit, making it pulse in awareness. Without pausing, Kyle slid between her folds. Aislinn shifted and spread her thighs wider. He traced her entrance, spreading the moisture gathered there.

"You're hot, Aislinn." He kissed the corner of her mouth. "Hot and wet." His palm pressed into her clit, sparking off a burst of energy.

She couldn't stand it. The touch was intense, but not enough. Aislinn lifted her hips.

"That's it, sweetheart. Move on me."

When she dropped down, a lean finger penetrated her and she gasped, waiting for the inevitable pain. There was none and she stared into Kyle's eyes.

"Keep going, baby. Let me see you come."

He slid in and out of her sheath and worked the tiny bundle of nerves with his thumb. The sensations spun tighter and tighter until she thought she'd literally explode.

Her orgasm rippled through her entire body. Aislinn bowed in his lap, throwing her head back with a moan while her womb clenched in an unending riot of pleasure. White lights sprang in her vision. Her clit spasmed on and on, and all the while the magical thumb never quit.

When it finally subsided, Aislinn's head was on the pillow behind her and she was draped across Kyle's lap. With his hand still firmly against her pussy, he played with her, lightly caressing her sopping wet lips.

Lungs heaving, Aislinn went limp and closed her eyes.

David had been wrong. She wasn't frigid. Not with Kyle. The man had played her body and made it sing with slow and steady fingers. Not an ounce of pressure, no forcing her to do something she didn't want. And she wanted. Oh my God, did she want.

Kyle leaned over and kissed her lips softly, no trace of the smugness she expected to see. Only tender emotion held her captive and made her tumble just a little bit further for him. Not in love. She could not be in love with Kyle Turner III.

ଓ଼ଃ

"You're beautiful, Aislinn." Kyle stabbed a forkful of salad and smiled over the way her cheeks reddened at his compliment. He meant beautiful in every sense of the word. When he'd made her come with his fingers, her cheeks had flushed, sweat had beaded on her forehead, plastering her bangs to the soft skin there. She had given herself to him wholeheartedly and been absolutely gorgeous in the throes of passion. And he'd only given her a small taste of how things could be between them.

"Thanks," she muttered.

"David's an ass."

"You don't have to tell me that." Aislinn laid her soup spoon down and picked the napkin up off her lap. "Does it make you feel like a big man to know you can do that to me?"

He snorted at the attitude. It was a defense mechanism for her.

"Nope." He sipped his wine. "But it makes me feel like King of the World to know I was the first."

"I'm sorry. I didn't mean for that to come out that way." She cocked her head. "Does it...happen like...well what you made happen"—she twisted her hand in the air—"every time?"

Kyle shrugged. "Probably not. It's something I work for though."

"With all your women?"

"I won't back off, sweetheart. No matter what you say. And I already told you, there hasn't been anyone since you came to work for me."

"Why?"

He reached across the table and took her hand in his. "I don't know," he answered honestly. "There's something about you, I guess." There was more to it than that, but he didn't know how to put into words what he felt. Protector, lover, cherisher, friend, anything she wanted him to be, he was ready.

"So who's Crystal if you haven't been with anyone, 'cause she sure calls a lot to not be in your life."

"Sweetheart, I do believe you're jealous."

She pulled her hand away and shook her head. "Am not."

He laughed. "You are." Might as well put her out of her misery. "Crystal is my sister. She's fifteen. Lives with our parents in Ohio."

Aislinn choked on the water she'd started drinking. When she could breathe again, she stared at him, obviously at a loss for words. He guessed it would throw anyone for a loop to know he had a fifteen-year-old sister. Because of his past, most of which was spent taking out some really bad people, Kyle kept his family life quiet.

Now he did so for a different reason, same end result. He didn't want anyone trying to get to him through his family. His parents were older, getting on in their years. Crystal had been more than a blessed surprise, to say the least.

"Fifteen?" she sputtered. "How old are you?"

"Thirty-two. My mom was in her forties when Crystal came along. And just so you know, I don't talk about Crystal to anyone."

Aislinn narrowed her eyes. "Why?"

"I've done a lot in my life, made a ton of money. There are any number of factions out there willing to use any means necessary to get to me. Any means now includes you too. I'll do anything in my power to keep the people closest to me from becoming a target for one of my enemies." He wasn't extraordinarily happy about the fact, but to have her in his life he'd make the changes to keep her safe. Hell, the security was already in place and had been since he'd learned of Tarkell.

"I thought you were out of the Special Forces."

"I am," he acknowledged, "but I more than pissed off a lot of ugly people during my time in. And a good majority of those people would probably love to get their payback anyway they can. Taking out a family member or loved one is an easy way to do it. An eye for an eye."

"Is that why TJ and Jonathan are always around you?"

What? He had to laugh silently. "Is that what they say about us at work?"

"Well it's obvious they work for you. Some kind of

bodyguards or something. You said yourself you'd pissed off a lot of people, and we all know you're worth *a ton of money.*"

This time he threw his head back and laughed out loud. He couldn't wait to tell his two best friends what everyone thought of them. Kyle took a long swallow of his water and smiled.

"No, they're not my bodyguards, although I'm sure they'd get a kick out of people thinking they were. TJ was our team leader. If any one of us were to be a bodyguard it would probably be me. Maybe Toad or Lazlow. But not TJ or Jonathan."

Aislinn gave him a curious look. "Then what do they do all day?"

"They're part owners of Turner Industries."

Her eyes bugged out.

"*Silent* owners," he stressed firmly, waiting for her to understand. Neither man wanted other people to know their exact involvement in the company, nor how much they were worth. They liked their lives simple. Adding money-hungry females into the equation only made things awkward. They may love women in every way possible but they wanted to find their third on their terms, not because a female was greedy. "TJ and Jon are the inventors I guess you'd say. Testers, too. They make sure the products are sound and work when they're supposed to. As for why they hang around the office so much?" He shrugged. "I think they have a vested interest in a certain female."

The mouthful of drink Aislinn had just sipped flew across the table at him.

Kyle calmly wiped the icy water from his face.

"Oh crap. I'm so sorry." Aislinn yanked her napkin from beneath her silverware and blotted everywhere the water spewed from her mouth had landed.

He chuckled. “Something I said?”

She nodded vigorously and changed the subject. He wondered if she knew the object of TJ and Jon’s desire was Christina.

“So all this time you’ve been watching me or having me watched—”

“I did a background check. An extensive one, yes, and I’ve had someone looking in on you now and then. Not watching. Making sure you were safe, more like,” he said returning to their original subject. “Of course there really hasn’t been a reason for any of my enemies to look at you until now because I haven’t gotten close to you before today.” He smiled, thinking about how close he’d actually gotten. It wouldn’t be long before his cock replaced his fingers in her tight, slick little pussy. Before he tasted the sweet heaven between her legs. Kyle shifted in his seat hoping to ease the pressure building in his groin.

“So why spend the money and time on me?”

Kyle straightened in his chair and cleared his throat. “You have one bastard of an ex. I saw what he did to you. I’ve heard the threats, talked to the police, and I know that he’s found you in every new city you’ve gone to. Maybe I just wanted you to be able to relax here.”

“Thank you.”

“You’re not mad?”

“I was. At first, in your office earlier.” Aislinn rubbed at the goose bumps Kyle saw on her arms from across the table.

“Cold?”

Her long hair swayed in its ponytail when she shook her head, and she busied herself with straightening her place setting. “But then I thought, why should I be mad when this man has gone out of his way to see to my safety? Now I’m grateful, because I think, in the back of my mind, I must have felt comfortable all this time. I no longer think of David every minute of every day, and I haven't been looking over my shoulder constantly which is something I've pretty much done nonstop since I started running." Her eyes were glistening when she looked up at him.

"A perfect segue."

"Huh?"

"Let's talk about your mind, sweetheart. What exactly is it you can do with that beautiful brain of yours."

Aislinn fidgeted. "I don't know what you're talking about."

"Right." He leaned forward so the other patrons couldn't hear them. "I wasn't lying when I said I know about everything, and you can't tell me you weren't surprised by my comment about the kitchen earlier today. I mean, it is why we're here tonight in the first place."

She gulped down the remainder of her water and searched for the waiter.

"I've talked to your mother, Aislinn."

Aislinn's gaze zeroed in on Kyle and her face paled. "You what?"

"I contacted her some time ago. She wasn't hard to find. Got the entire story from her. She's very happy to keep in touch so she knows you're safe."

"God. Do you know how big of a bastard you sound like right now?"

Their waiter arrived and placed the entrées they'd ordered, then asked them if they cared for anything else. Kyle ordered another bottle of wine knowing he'd opened an ugly can of worms. Keeping her from speaking to her mother had been a bastard of a thing to do, but he had his reasons.

Aislinn shook off the waiter. He promised to return to refill her water and took his leave. "Your mother asked me not to tell you, Aislinn."

"Mama wouldn't do that."

"She did." He pulled his cell phone from his pocket and dialed Darla Campbell's number. It was past time for mother and daughter to talk.

"You talk to her so much you know her phone number?" she hissed.

"Photographic memory," he said, listening to the phone ring on the other end.

"Hello?"

"Darla, it's Kyle Turner." He gazed across the table at Aislinn. Her whole body was a mass of vibrating nerves. Her nostrils flared with every inhalation and her eyes were as wide as the saucers on the table.

"Mr. Turner. What is it? Has something happened?"

"Actually, something has happened, but I think I'll let you talk to Aislinn herself."

"Oh my God," Darla breathed, a hitch catching the "God" in her throat.

Kyle held the phone out to Aislinn. For long seconds she stared at the phone as if it might come to life and bite her. Then with tentative fingers she reached out and took it from his fingers. He heard Darla on the other end, "Aislinn? Baby? Hello?"

"Mama?" she whispered and covered the sob that tore from her throat with her hand.

Chapter Four

Her mama was on the phone. She was talking to her mother. For the first time in so long.

"Oh Lord, girl, it's so good to hear your voice, baby."

"Mama." Aislinn swallowed past the lump in her throat. Kyle stabbed into the humongous steak he'd ordered like nothing was out of the ordinary. She eyed her own bowl of Pasta con Broccoli and decided she would be happy never seeing food again. Her stomach dipped and her heart clenched.

"Oh, baby, I miss you so much."

"Me too," she mouthed, unable to speak the words out loud. A tear slipped down her cheek. Kyle handed her a napkin. She took it and wiped her face and nose which had started to run.

"You're safe, Aislinn? Nothing's happened, has it? I told Mr. Turner not to tell you we'd been talking, honey. I didn't want you to think I was putting you in jeopardy again. He assured me that whenever he called we were on a secure line and that no one could trace it. God, no one did, did they? He hasn't found you again, has he? Please tell me you aren't having to move again."

"Mama," Aislinn laughed, "no, I'm still here, he hasn't been seen." She sought Kyle's eyes and held his gaze. "I had a vision, Mama, and Kyle seems to know all about it."

His cheeks and jaw worked as he chewed, sending an odd little shiver deep into her belly. Sensation started to return, taking over the numbness that had formed the second she'd heard her mother's voice. Kyle nodded. Yep. He knew all right. Everything. Something very few people knew about.

David had known. It was one of the reasons he'd been so intent on keeping her. To use her as his own little sideshow.

"I told him," her mother admitted without an ounce of remorse. She must have trusted Kyle implicitly to share their generations-old secret with him. The fact eased Aislinn's mind more than anything Kyle could have said. Her mother had the same gift, as did her grandmother and great-grandmother and all the women before her.

The second sight passed down through the first daughter of the first daughter. Along with the flaming red hair and green eyes. Lucky Aislinn.

"He had to know if he was going to protect you at all, Aislinn. He's a man of honor and of his word. I believe he will do anything to keep you safe."

The same man devouring his still mooing Porterhouse like he'd never eaten before *would* do anything. Aislinn believed this also. Like she'd told him minutes ago, if she hadn't felt safe in his vicinity, she probably wouldn't have stayed so long here, nor would she be relaxing her position of no more men.

She thought back to when they were in her house, with her stretched out over his lap, his fingers deep inside her pussy and the resulting explosive climax. Her first. She suddenly wanted to feel it again. Her cheeks flamed and one of his eyebrows rose. Aislinn dipped her head but felt that his gaze didn't leave her.

"Besides, I've *seen* him, baby. I know he's the man you need."

She snorted. "The man I need, Mama? Seeing him in a

vision isn't the same as meeting him in person. What if I'm not ready for another man?" A lightning bolt was surely going to strike her dead any second. Kyle's fork landed loudly against his plate and she jerked her head up. His eyes were narrowed into deadly slits, making her nipples harden and ache. She hadn't really meant for him to hear that. Hell, she hadn't meant to say it. So why had she?

"You're a liar, Aislinn Campbell," her mother scoffed. "Listen to your heart, it will tell you where you need to go."

"Like it did with David?" she cried.

"Oh, honey. No part of your heart was involved with that rat bastard. I'm not sure what attracted you to him but it most definitely was not your heart."

"Maybe I just have horrible taste in men."

Now Kyle slammed the napkin from his lap onto the table. Cutlery jumped, clanging against the china. He licked his teeth and she wondered if it was her he'd rather be eating than the steak he'd already worked halfway through. The thought was a little more appealing than it should be.

"No, you don't. David had some kind of pull over you, Aislinn. But he's good and gone now and you need to get on with your life. Speaking of which, where are you two that you're together so late in the evening?"

"We're"—she cleared her throat—"at dinner."

"Ooh, dinner. As in on a date?"

She glanced at Kyle again. He was still glaring at her, fisting the napkin in one hand and the wicked-looking knife in the other.

"Not a date. We're discussing—"

"We are on a date, Aislinn. Gimme that phone, woman." Kyle reached out and snatched the phone from her hand.

"Hey," Aislinn squeaked, but she couldn't hold back the smile. It felt...nice, she guessed, to get that kind of reaction from Kyle.

"Darla, your daughter and I are on a date," he said, promising sensual retribution that made her toes curl, while giving her more of the evil eye, "to discuss the fact she's seen me in a vision getting murdered in a kitchen. It is a *date*."

She heard her mama laughing through the phone.

"Oh, my," Darla sighed, still laughing. "Kyle. May I call you Kyle? I most certainly know you are on a date. Aislinn is not the only one who can see things. I just wanted to hear her say it." She chuckled again. "She's a tough nut to crack though and David hasn't made things easy for you."

"Yes, ma'am, I know that."

"Right. Well then, I think I need to get off the phone so you can finish your date. How's your steak, dear?"

Aislinn had heard it all and she got the smug satisfaction of seeing him whip the phone off his ear and stare at it, then his steak, then back at the phone as if it had grown horns.

"My mother's talent is far more advanced than mine," she explained and stuck her tongue out at him.

"It's fine," he answered Darla calmly.

"Good. Good. I'll say goodbye now."

"Goodbye, Mama," Aislinn called, loud enough her mother could hear.

"Ma'am." Kyle nodded and flipped the lid closed before sticking the phone back in its holster. "You happy now?"

Was she happy? Couldn't he tell? She was ecstatic, bouncing in her seat. Hearing her mother's voice was a balm to her senses.

She tilted her head and studied him as he picked up his

fork again. "Thank you."

He eyed her over his wineglass, took a sip, set it carefully down and said, "You're welcome." His face radiated sincerity and her heart thumped. This man was absolutely the polar opposite of David.

David had told her what she'd wanted to hear. After pondering what had gone wrong in the relationship, she'd realized everything David had done to her had been brainwashing, plain and simple. Post escape—because it had been an escape from the bastard—it had taken her a long time to come to terms with her inability to see through his exterior to the man he truly was.

Kyle was different. At least, so far he hadn't tried to act anything like David, who in hindsight had basically stalked her from the moment they met. At first she'd seen him as sweet, showering her with gifts and taking her to shows and dinner all the time. She'd thought it was because he liked spending time with her. Instead, he'd wanted to mold her into his perfect idea of a wife. It wasn't until they were married his true colors had come out.

Kyle pointed at her plate with his fork. "Eat. Your food's getting cold."

She looked down at the creamy pasta and her stomach growled. Kyle snorted and she laughed. A few minutes ago she'd thought she'd choke if she took a bite, now she found herself ravenous.

Scooping up a forkful, she savored the richness. She'd never eaten here before, couldn't afford to. It was a different taste than any other Pasta con Broccoli dish she'd had before. Almost had a kick to it. She shrugged and dug in.

"Good?"

Aislinn nodded. "It's different," she said, echoing her

thoughts.

"You should try the lasagna next time, it's excellent. What they're known for."

She raised a brow. "Next time?"

"Yes." His eyes begged her to disagree. He dug into his steak again. "You love your mother."

"Well, yeah, don't you love your mother?"

"Sure, but you have a different relationship with your mom then I do with mine. My parents worked hard all their lives providing for us and doing whatever they could to give my sister and me the best life possible. She cried when I told her I wanted to join the Navy and be a SEAL. She supported me and the pride was evident, but deep down I knew she hated my decision."

"What mother wouldn't?" Hers probably. Darla Campbell would have already seen it in a vision, along with any outcomes and would have kissed her daughter on the forehead and told her to go forth and make a difference. God only knows why her mother hadn't seen the disaster David would become. "Wondering if you were safe every second of the day while you were gone must have been sheer torture for her."

"I'm sure it was," he agreed, "but I get the feeling you had an entirely different upbringing. And I can see you being much closer to your mother than I am to mine."

"Maybe that's because I'm a girl."

Fork halfway to his mouth, he paused. "My sister doesn't get along with Mom."

"Your sister is fifteen. I didn't get along with mine either at fifteen."

"Good point." His eyes twinkled and the corners of his mouth turned up. "Now. Tell me about this kitchen."

Aislinn choked on the piece of broccoli she'd been chewing. The man needed the word persistent tattooed on his forehead. He already knew about the clairvoyance but that didn't make it any easier to talk about.

"Maybe it was just a dream."

"Do you always dream of killing off your employers?"

"I bet more than three-quarters of the world dream of killing the people they work for."

"Perhaps," he spoke around a bite of potato. "But you don't *just* dream. I've watched you at work."

Her face paled as she searched her memory for anything she might have said or done at work. No specific instances came to mind.

"You're very good at covering yourself, and the couple of times you weren't capable, I stepped in. Don't worry, sweetheart."

"Don't worry? Not many people outside of my mother know what I can do, and I'd kinda like to keep it that way," she said through gritted teeth. No sense in letting the entire restaurant in on her secret. "You have no idea how people treat you when they know. I become some kind of carnival freak show."

"I don't—"

"Not to mention all the people who want to test you and poke you and prod you like a pincushion."

"Ais—"

"And then there are the people who'd like to lock you up in a loony bin on the premise of, 'We don't want you to hurt yourself', all the while patting you on the back and twirling their finger in a circle beside their ear. So you'll have to excuse me if I worry about people getting too close."

Kyle sat back in his chair and studied her for a moment.

She felt like a newfound species.

"Are you done?"

Aislinn straightened from her position leaning over the table so she wouldn't have to shout. A quick glance around showed she hadn't succeeded. Several patrons whispered and stared.

Great.

"I can honestly say I've never seen the temper. I think I like it." Kyle looked ready to drag her out of here. His eyes glowed with heated promises.

"You would," she muttered.

"For the record, I don't think any of those things about you. Okay, I'm lying, I don't want you to hurt yourself, but I promise not to lock you away. Keep eating so everyone will stop looking at you."

She did. The food was good, no reason it should go to waste because she'd had a hissy fit.

"If you've seen something pertaining to me and, oh I don't know, my death, then yes, I want to know about it. I'm not ready to die, sweetheart. I haven't gotten the chance to sink my cock so deep inside you, you don't know where you end and I begin yet. Trust me, that time is coming."

Aislinn sucked in a breath at his outrageously sincere comment as he looked at her from beneath his lashes.

"What makes you think I'll allow you to?" Christ, her pussy creamed just thinking about him stretching her and getting as close as two people could. She squeezed her thighs together, but she was afraid nothing would dissipate the ache there except the man sitting across from her.

"If you think it won't happen, maybe you do belong in a loony bin. Right now, however, I'm more interested in how I'm going to die."

"You are infuriating."

He grinned. "Thank you."

She buried her head in her hands. "I give up."

"I knew you would."

"There isn't much to tell," Aislinn capitulated.

"Anything would be more than the cryptic email saying 'stay out of the kitchen'."

He was laughing at her! She glanced up, her eyes narrowed, only to find no sign of a smile on his face. "What did you want me to say? I predict you will die in a kitchen by the knife of a madman in the very near future?"

Kyle pointed at her. "Anything spoken to my face would have been better than the email, sweetheart. The knife of a madman, huh?"

"And if I had said that, TJ and Jonathan would have wrapped me in a straitjacket the minute the words left my mouth."

"And I already told you, TJ and Jon aren't my bodyguards."

"Can I get you anything else? Perhaps some dessert?" the waiter interrupted, his gaze straying to her mostly uneaten plate of food. "Or a box?" He looked worried. "Was there something wrong with the dish, ma'am?"

Guilty color stained her cheeks. "No, not at all. I had a...I just haven't been able to eat it yet, thank you."

His shoulders relaxing visibly, he nodded before turning to Kyle. "Another glass of wine, sir?"

"No, I'm good. Thank you."

The waiter nodded again and turned, leaving Aislinn and Kyle alone.

"Continue," Kyle urged.

Aislinn sighed and rubbed at a spot of pain blooming at her temple. It was congruent with the one forming in her tummy. "It was dark, but there was enough moonlight to see the knife. The intruder was wearing all black and you were…not."

"Not? What am I wearing?"

She gulped. "Very little."

"Yeah?" he said with a smirk. "How little?"

Blowing her bangs off her forehead, Aislinn held on to her temper. It turned him on more than anything anyways, and wouldn't get her very far in the current situation. He was starting to piss her off by not being serious. He said he believed her, so why wasn't he concerned?

"Come on, tell me how little I was wearing," he whispered, hovering over his empty plate.

"Boxers," she ground out. "Is that all you care about?"

"Boxers, huh?" His face turned serious. "No, but sweetheart, there's nothing I can do about it except follow your advice and stay out of kitchens for a while. I'll do anything you tell me to concerning this."

Her shoulders drooped. There really wasn't anything else she could do. If he believed her, it had to be enough.

"Okay?" he asked, concern lacing his tone.

She bit her lip and nodded.

"I did warn you what I'd do if you didn't stop biting that lip, didn't I?" he growled.

Chapter Five

Kyle parked the car in Aislinn's driveway and studied the small ranch-style house. The porch light was on. Nothing looked disturbed. Even the light he remembered seeing on in what was probably a bathroom window still glowed.

Didn't make him want to leave her here though. "Come home with me," he asked again, reaching over and dragging her closer with a hand around the back of her neck. He caressed her forehead with his lips and inhaled the strawberry scent of her hair. This made the third time he'd tried to convince her to stay the night with him. It killed him that she kept saying no.

She shook her head and peered up at him. "I can't," she sighed. "Not yet." Aislinn pulled away and the soft strands of her hair trailed along his arm. "I..."

"What?"

"It's just too fast."

Throwing his head back, Kyle groaned. "It's been six months."

"For you maybe. We haven't been seeing each other, Kyle. I still feel weird because I just had dinner with my boss. For me our relationship's only like six hours old."

He snorted. "You can't tell me you've felt nothing all this time. I see it when I walk in the room, sweetheart." He traced her cheek with his thumb. "Your breath hitches"—he moved down and laid his fingers on her chest—"here, just like this." Kyle smiled at her sharp inhalation before covering her breast. "Your nipples harden into stiff peaks, the way they're stabbing into my palm now."

Aislinn bit her lip. Her eyes slid shut and her back arched into his touch. He wasn't lying about her response to him. Getting her to see it and believe it and to forget everything in her past was the key.

"Your pussy creams," he whispered, feathering kisses on her nose and lips.

"I can't." Her voice wobbled in desire and her thighs clenched with the thought.

He smelled her in the confines of the car and wanted to spread her legs and dive between them to feast on the offering he knew he'd find there. They didn't serve any dessert as good as what lay nestled at the juncture of her thighs.

Kyle rubbed his forehead on hers. Close but no cigar. If he pushed any harder, he was afraid he might lose her. She wasn't going anywhere. Not tonight anyway. Tomorrow morning he'd show up bright and early, ready to ease her more fully into his life. Spend the day with her, maybe surprise her and buy a birthday present before his annual Fourth of July party tomorrow night. Anything her little heart desired. And he was getting sappy.

"Fine," he gave in, "I'm going in with you. I want to make sure you get in okay before I go." And give himself time to walk off the erection painfully pressed against his fly.

"But, I—"

"Don't argue with me on this, Aislinn. You won't win." He threw the door open and stepped out, sucking in a lungful of night air to replace the scent of her skin and her sopping pussy.

Tonight would be long and restless, and tomorrow probably longer because of the party. She'd be there, but he wouldn't have much time alone with her. Not with the entire Turner Industries staff hanging around.

Kyle didn't care about the attention they'd garner by being close, but Aislinn would and he wasn't willing to risk her bolting.

He walked around the hood of the car, already sticky with sweat from the early July heat. The impatient woman had one foot out her door before he reached her side.

"I'll be fine, Kyle."

"And I'm going to check the house out." Shutting the door, he directed her up the path with a hand on the small of her back. He felt her shiver.

"Don't tell me you're cold."

"Uh-uh." She shook her head and stumbled, nearly losing her boxed-up pasta.

Kyle reached out and grabbed her shoulders, pulling her into his chest. "Whoa, you okay?"

"Yeah." She rubbed at her temple, something he'd seen her do earlier at dinner. "Just got a headache."

"All right then, let's get you inside and into bed." Bye-bye erection. Now he knew the cure. Let the woman he loved not feel well.

Love? Damn. Did he love her? Kyle took the key she dug out of her purse and unlocked the front door. Pushing it open, he stood for a moment, listening for anything out of place. He ushered her inside and propped her against the wall.

"Stay. For me, please. I'll be right back. Yes?"

She nodded, eyeing him as if he'd lost his mind. Kyle shrugged it off. This was part of his nature. Ingrained from his years as a SEAL. The need to watch his back and that of his family and friends would probably never fade.

"Don't be long," she whispered. "I'm tired."

He growled at her. "Don't move."

He heard the loud snap of her finger and thumb and then, "Oh, shit."

"What?" He swung back around, hands fisted, ready to drop someone when he saw her expression was really one of a light bulb going off in her head.

"Umm... My room. Uh, yeah, the clothes, my fault. Sorry. Just didn't want you to think someone had been in there."

He chuckled. "Are you a slob, Aislinn?"

"Something like that," she grumbled.

It didn't take long to go through her house. Not near as long as it took for him to stop staring at the massive amount of clothes piled on her floor. Slob was an understatement. Everything she owned had to be thrown on the heap. What the hell had she been doing? The rest of her house hadn't looked this way.

Along the way, he stopped in the bathroom off her bedroom and grabbed a couple of aspirin from the very precise medicine cabinet and a glass of water.

"Here." Kyle handed her the glass and relieved her of the to-go box before giving her the pills, then turned to the kitchen to stuff her dinner in the fridge.

"You are a god," she moaned.

"I heard that."

"As if you didn't know it," she muttered.

"I heard that too," he called over his shoulder and tried to figure out a place to stash the box in her crowded refrigerator.

"Whatever."

By the time he came back into the room, she was gone. He traipsed down the hallway to find her slumping on her bed, leaving the mess for later. Must be a killer headache. She closed her eyes and sighed.

Kyle put his hands on his hips. "That's it."

She glanced at him from one eye. "What?"

"Come home with me."

"No."

"Lord you're stubborn."

Her smile was laced with pain. "My mama says stubborn is my middle name. Must have something to do with the red hair."

"I don't want to leave you here when you're not feeling well."

"I'll be fine." She grabbed the back of her neck and rolled it on her shoulders. "It's a headache for heaven's sake."

"Do you have them a lot?"

"Only when I'm about to have a vision," she answered with complete nonchalance.

Kyle counted on his years of training to keep him from exploding. "God damn it, Aislinn—"

"I'm kidding, Kyle. It's a headache, that's all. Everyone gets them. A good night's sleep and I'll be good as new."

He took a deep breath. What else could he do? Sleep on her couch. In his car. No. She was right. Staying would only show her he didn't think she could handle herself. He didn't want to betray the trust they were developing.

"If you're sure?" He couldn't resist trying one more time.

She yawned. "Positive." A second later she was stretching out on top of her quilt-covered bed, still fully clothed.

He couldn't help but smile. "Don't mind me, I'll see my way out."

"Kyle?"

"Yeah, baby?"

"Could I have...?"

Damn if her eyes weren't begging him for something. His cock stirred to life. If she even hinted she wanted him to stay he'd be a goner because no way could he lie with her in a bed and not touch her. And from the distressed look on her face, there was no way he could do anything but hold her.

"Can you have what?"

Her gaze met his, the slightly glazed look in her eyes making him feel like a sex-crazed heel.

"A good-night kiss?" she whispered huskily.

Shit. Shit. He swallowed, half afraid he wouldn't be able to stop if he got that close to her, but damned if he'd walk out when she clearly wasn't used to asking for even something as simple as a kiss.

He leaned over her warm body and pushed the bangs off her forehead with two fingers. She turned into his touch with a sigh.

"Did you take those pills, sweetheart?"

"Yes, Dad."

He snorted and placed a chaste kiss on her cheek. "I'm feeling anything but dad-ish right now, baby, and I'm trying very hard to keep my hands off your body."

Eyes widening, Aislinn sucked in a breath and licked her lips. He could have kicked himself.

"Thank you."

"For what?" Kyle inhaled her scent.

"For not pushing it."

"We will make love, Aislinn. That's a promise."

Eyes wide, she pursed her lips. "I know."

He nuzzled the soft skin between her jaw and shoulder, licking and nibbling his way to her earlobe and down to her mouth, where he met her open, eager lips. Her admission was all he needed. She wanted it too. He tangled his tongue with hers, rubbing along the velvet length, tasting her sweetness. It would have to do for tonight.

Breathing heavily, Aislinn retreated. He wondered if she realized her hands were tucked into the open collar of his shirt. Standing slowly, he unfolded the afghan from the foot of her bed and covered her with it.

"Tomorrow morning, Aislinn. I will be here." He made it a fact, not a question.

"I'll see you then."

He nodded once. "Sleep tight, sweetheart. Oh, and one more thing." Kyle pulled his wallet out of his back pocket and retrieved a business card. "My home phone number. Call it if you need anything in the night. *Anything*, Aislinn."

"I will."

"You better," he grunted and turned to leave before he was tempted to stay, whether she wanted him to or not.

ଔ଼

The vomiting started about a half an hour after Kyle left. One minute she was sleeping, the next vicious cramps seized her stomach. Aislinn had barely made it to the toilet the first time. She hadn't the second time—ten minutes later. Using a towel, she'd sopped up the mess and thrown it in the bathtub to deal with later.

Now she was on her fourth trip in a total of twenty minutes. This wasn't the flu. Her stomach clamped down and lights burst behind her tightly squeezed eyes. She'd never felt this bad in her entire life. Curled up in the fetal position on the bathroom floor, she wondered if she was even capable of making it back into bed. Or if she wanted to try. Another wave of nausea struck. Aislinn bucked into a kneeling position and dry heaved violently.

Slumping to the floor once more, she tried to remember what she'd eaten during the day. Lunch with Christina at their normal café. She'd had the chicken tortilla soup, same as every other time. Dinner with Kyle tonight. The pasta. Aside from its spiciness...

Her stomach revolted but she couldn't find the energy to move from her spot. Her belly was empty anyway. Tears sprang to her eyes. Sweat plastered her hair to her face and her blouse to her body. She needed help. And the phone was so far away. She glared across the expanse of bathroom and bedroom to the portable phone on her nightstand.

Who could she call? Christina was her only hope. She couldn't move. Didn't want to move for fear it would set off another spasm. Breathing through her nose, Aislinn closed her eyes. A chill on top of her sweat-drenched body sent a shiver through her.

After another fierce round of dry heaves, she decided she had to try to call someone. At this moment 911 was looking like a beautiful option.

She crawled, inching her way over the mile-wide distance to the nightstand. At the foot of the bed she had to stop to puke and pressed her head against the cool wood of the footboard.

She was dying. From the inside out. She'd never get to

make love to Kyle. The swirly pattern of the rug beneath her danced and moved. She just needed a little nap. Collapsing face first, Aislinn did her best to stay awake. Not hard with the intense pain seizing her belly. The coarse fabric of the rug abraded her cheek adding immensely to her discomfort. She gauged the remaining space between her and help. Her vision swam and she feared in a few minutes she'd pass out without making any call.

Garnering all the strength she had left, Aislinn army crawled to the stand and reached up to feel for the phone. Finally finding it, she pulled it off. A small piece of paper fluttered down from the top of the table and landed on her nose before sliding to the ground.

She groaned as if the paper had been a rock shot from a cannon.

Kyle's business card.

Aislinn fumbled the card and squinted at the rapidly blurring numbers. His home phone. Call me anytime, he'd said.

Dialing the tiny buttons proved nearly impossible for her shaky fingers but at last the call went through. Too weak to lift the phone to her ear, she left it on the floor.

"Hello?" Kyle's rough voice answered on the first ring.

She sobbed in relief. "Kyle?"

ଔଓ

Christ, he'd never been so scared. Hearing Aislinn's panicked voice on the end of the line had stopped his heart. One word. Kyle. It was all she'd said before going silent.

He'd shouted through the phone and gotten no response. The line was still open though. He knew because he'd tried calling her several times on his cell with no luck.

Kyle took the turn onto her street with a screech of tires. Her house was dark and quiet when he pulled into the driveway behind her Civic. Having no idea what was happening not an hour after he'd left her, he'd grabbed his SIG from its case and bolted, prepared to take anyone out who got in his way.

He peeked through the living room window where the drapes didn't quite meet. Nothing. As much as he wanted to bust the door down and go in guns blazing, he couldn't put her in that kind of danger. Kyle worked his way around the house. He saw nothing out of the ordinary. No clues as to what the problem might be.

Had she let someone in the house? Had David found her again? Was he too late?

His stomach twisted in knots. This was worse than any mission he'd ever gone on with his SEAL team. This was personal. Training instinct kicked in by the time he got to the back door. Taking a deep breath, Kyle closed his eyes and focused on what needed to be done.

Using the butt of the gun, he punched out a pane of glass from the door leading to the kitchen. Hopefully the tinkling of glass wouldn't alert anyone inside to his presence. He could have used more stealth but had a feeling there wasn't time for detailed planning.

Kyle reached in and unlocked both the deadbolt and the knob's lock. He remembered seeing a chain lock too when he'd been in the kitchen earlier. Her smart, extra-added safety measure was a tad unfortunate for Kyle. He turned his wrist and pushed further into the small opening, hissing as a shard of glass cut into his forearm.

Ignoring the pain, he groped for the chain and slid it free. A second later he stood in the dark kitchen listening for the slightest sound. He got it. Down the hall towards her bedroom. He searched his brain for what he'd heard. Heaving was the only thing he could come up with. No other noises intruded.

Son of a bitch. Aislinn was sick and he'd been outside her house in SEAL mode. Stuffing the gun in his jeans at the small of his back, Kyle slid the deadbolt home and raced to her room.

"Shit." He dropped to his knees and carefully turned the woman he loved onto her back. "Sweetheart. Talk to me." He patted her pale, sweaty cheek and her eyelashes fluttered.

"Aislinn," he said with more force.

She groaned and tried to pull her knees to her chest.

"Christ. Come on, baby." He yanked the quilt off her bed and after covering her with it, lifted her into his arms.

He kicked the front door closed with his heel. Halfway down the walk Aislinn jackknifed in his arms, rapping his chin with her forehead and crying out in pain. She retched, only nothing came out.

"How the fuck long you been doing this, baby?" he growled. Since the second he'd left her asleep on her bed most likely, if she only had dry heaves now. She cried and turned her head into his chest, gripping his shirt with a weak fist.

Kyle yanked open the car door, placed his precious burden on the passenger seat and jogged to the other side. A quick phone call later and the emergency room knew he was on the way.

Chapter Six

Kyle paced the cubicle Aislinn had been placed in, hands on hips. He'd filled out paperwork, listing her as his wife to hurry things along. The ploy had worked. Or maybe it was the fact he was Kyle Turner III and they knew any lack of insurance on Aislinn's part wouldn't be an issue. Who knew? The end result was that she'd been brought into the ER without having to wait her turn in the waiting room. Or maybe it had been the look on his face. Could have also been the fact she had puked three times while he stood holding her at the triage desk. They'd offered him a wheelchair but he'd refused. Instead they'd rushed her into their present cubicle.

The doctor had taken blood, inquired whether she'd been out of the country, asked what she'd eaten lately, and finally—after Kyle had impatiently answered *almost* every question without strangling the man—had given Aislinn a shot of something for the nausea. It seemed to be working. The last ten minutes her stomach had been quiet. In the car she hadn't gone three without her tummy erupting. She'd scared the shit out of him.

Not even a buddy of his who'd gotten some nasty bug down in an undisclosed South American location had been as sick as Aislinn.

Kyle had a pretty good idea what had caused what the doctor had determined to be food poisoning. In the morning he'd send TJ to her house to retrieve the pasta and find out what the fuck was actually in it.

The restaurant they'd eaten in was well known and catered to the wealthy. Kyle had a hard time believing they'd made a bad batch of pasta. It could have happened but after dwelling on the possibility the last half hour, he was not inclined to go that route. Not when he knew there were people capable of deliberately doing him harm by any means. Since it was a little early for any of his possible enemies to have targeted Aislinn, he had a feeling David Tarkell had succeeded in finding her yet again.

From what he'd seen at her house, he didn't think David had entered her dwelling space. Yet. He had two options, he thought, swiping her bangs off her forehead. She turned into his touch on a sigh.

One, he could try and convince her to stay with him for the next couple of days so his men would have time to get out there and find the bastard before he was able to get to Aislinn again. Two, he could tell her what he thought was happening and hope like hell she didn't panic and run. He liked the former plan much better.

"Mr. Turner."

Kyle turned to the doctor.

"I'm going to release your wife into your care with this prescription." He finished scribbling on the tablet he held, ripped off the top sheet and handed it to Kyle. "It should help her get some rest. The shot will last several more hours."

Kyle nodded. He'd glue her to his bed if he had to, to make sure she got the rest.

"If you've got any idea what she ate that might have caused

this, I'd like to know, so we can keep our eyes open for any more possible cases. This kind of thing has to be reported so the FDA can intervene."

"I'm not sure where she ate today," Kyle lied again, sticking to his original answer. "I'll ask her about it when she wakes up."

The doctor accepted his answer. "If she starts vomiting again in the morning, get her in to her personal physician."

He'll come to the house, trust me. "I will. Thank you." He shook hands with the man.

The doctor turned Kyle's arm one way then the other. "That's a pretty nasty scratch on your arm there. Do you want me to look at it?"

Kyle stared at the blood on his arm. Where had...the glass. "No. It's just a scratch." He couldn't tell him it was from the glass shattering when he'd broken into her house. He was supposed to be her husband.

"Give it a good wash and a dab of antibiotic cream then."

"I will." Kyle watched him walk away before turning back to Aislinn.

"Aislinn, sweetheart." He rubbed her cheek with the back of his knuckles. She was completely wrung out and didn't even stir.

He had her in his bed, right where she belonged, within an hour.

ଔଓ

Aislinn sighed and turned onto her side, snuggling into the pillow that smelled so much like Kyle she had to smile. She inhaled his scent again, loving the dream currently occupying her sleep.

"Nah, she's still asleep. I need you to go over and get the pasta though."

She lifted an eyelid. There, staring back at her was Kyle, sprawled in a big overstuffed armchair, legs stretched out wide in front of him.

"Hey, one eye," he said, giving her a wink. "No, she just peeked at me. I want you to analyze it ASAP."

Who was he talking to and why was he in her room? She lifted her head, groaned and looked around in confusion.

Not her room. One she'd never seen before and not one generic enough to be a hotel.

"It's mine," Kyle stated, flipping his cell closed on his cheek.

"How did..."

"You get here?" he finished. "You don't remember last night?"

Aislinn closed her eyes and laid her head on the pillow. His pillow. The reason it smelled so much like him. Her stomach growled, bringing everything that had happened back.

Mortified, she buried her face, hiding it from him. How many times had she puked? How many times had he seen her puke? Half the night was a blur, the other half she wanted to be. On top of it all, he'd carried her everywhere and she specifically remembered at one point upchucking on him. There could be nothing worse in life than throwing up on the man you were falling in love with.

She took another quick peek at him. A roguish grin split his lips. Fabulous. He thought this was funny. Even funnier would be when she peed on his bed. The pressing need was making itself more than evident. No matter what, she'd have to get out of his bed and use the bathroom.

Aislinn groaned again. She didn't want to move. It was cozy and warm tucked under his covers.

"Need to get up, sweetheart?" He chuckled.

"I'm glad you find this so hysterical," she mumbled, turning to face him.

In a flash he was by her side, mere inches away. Tender fingers brushed her hair from her face.

"There is nothing funny about what you went through last night, and I promise I'll get to the bottom of it."

"To the bottom of what?" What the hell was he talking about? She got sick, called him and ended up here. What was there to get to the bottom of?

"Aislinn, last night wasn't a bout of flu. You were poisoned."

She sat up gingerly, aided by Kyle's hands on her shoulders.

"Go slow," he said.

"What do you mean, like, *food* poisoning?"

He shrugged. "My guess is there was something in your pasta. Thank God you didn't eat the whole thing. If you'd had more, I can't imagine you'd be with me right now."

"So, what, the sauce was bad? There's not much in Pasta con Broccoli that can go bad, Kyle."

He shook his head. "No. I don't think it had anything to do with the restaurant. I don't know much right now, but I have people looking into it."

Confused, she looked at him, trying to figure out what he wasn't saying. If the food wasn't tainted then the only other option would be that someone had done it on...

"You think David did this?" she whispered.

Kyle rubbed his hands up and down her arms in a reassuring gesture. It did little to ward the chill quickly taking over. So much for finding a safe place. When would she be free of her ex? Never? Would she have to look over her shoulder for the rest of her life?

"I'm not saying anything, Aislinn."

"But it's what you're thinking."

"He's a possibility, yes." He wiped a thumb across her bottom lip when she sucked it in to bite on it nervously. "Hey. Let's get you up. Use the toilet and I'll run a bath, since I don't think you should stand in the shower when you're this weak. You can slide into a shirt of mine afterwards, and if you're really good, I'll bring you some soup to try to get down."

She wrinkled her nose even as her eyes filled with tears.

"Ah, baby." He laid her head on his shoulder and stroked her hair.

When was the last time someone had taken care of her? Probably not since her teenage years. And it sure the hell hadn't been a man.

"I won't let him hurt you." He pulled back and took her face between his hands. "I want you to stay here with me until we find him."

It wasn't a request and she wasn't stupid. Staying alone was the furthest from a good idea as she could get. She nodded and he swiped away a tear from her cheek with his thumb.

"Thank God," he rasped. "I thought you'd be one of those independent types who thought you could do it all on your own."

She laughed and sniffed. "I can't handle him on my own." Aislinn looked him straight in the eye and took a leap of faith. "And I don't want to anymore."

"Fuck, baby, you don't know how glad I am to hear you say that. So. A bath?"

"Definitely."

"Let's hit it then." He stood and scooped her off the bed.

"Put me down," she squealed.

"Pfft. Put a little more strength behind your request."

"I can't," she murmured and settled her head on his shoulder. She loved being in his arms. He made her feel cherished, not like an object, and she was starting to think she'd never be the same without him.

"All right." Kyle set her on the commode. "Can you sit there on your own?" He steadied her when she tilted to the side.

Her arms and legs felt like wiggly Jell-O and the shag rug in front of the most gigantic tub she'd ever seen looked more than inviting. Soft and fluffy. Maybe she needed another nap.

"Stay," he said, propping her against the toilet's tank.

She snorted. "I'm not a dog."

His gaze roamed hotly over every inch of her body and his nostrils flared. She squirmed under the scrutiny.

"No, you are certainly not a dog, sweetheart."

He looked like he was going to step closer and strip her bare of the... Aislinn stared at the unfamiliar shirt she wore, plucking at it. "Hmm."

"Yes, I did it. I undressed you and stuffed your pretty little body into a clean shirt. You wanted to sleep in the disgusting clothes you were wearing?" One of his eyebrows lifted, daring her to say yes. He crossed his muscle-packed arms before propping a hip on the sink.

His groin was at eye level to her. Aislinn licked her lips and nibbled on the lower one. She knew what lurked behind the zipper of his fly. Had felt it pressed along her lower back anyway. Besides, all's fair in love and war, right? He'd obviously gotten a sneak peek at her when he'd changed her clothes sometime in the night. Why shouldn't she get to have a little—

"Hey. Honey." He snapped his fingers until she jerked her gaze to his. "Not gonna happen. I'd have you worn out after one kiss, you're so weak."

She curled her top lip in contempt and her shoulders sagged. He was right, damn it. Kyle stepped out of temptation's reach and started the water in the Jacuzzi-style tub. Soon steam rose from the bubbling water and her mouth practically watered. She couldn't wait to sink into its depths, letting those jets pound every bit of her body. Every bit.

God, she groaned silently. She'd spent all night puking, but her sex didn't seem to care.

"So are you gonna go or what?"

The man had grown a second head for sure. "Not with you in here," she said with as much indignant menace as she could muster.

Kyle sighed. "I've already seen all of you."

"So? You haven't seen me go to the bathroom." Her cheeks had to be fire engine red.

He winced at her shrill outburst. "Fine. But I'm going to be right outside that door until I hear you get in the tub. Someone's gotta come rescue your ass when you fall on your face," he muttered, stomping out of the bathroom like a petulant child.

She should have swallowed her pride and let him help her, she thought five minutes later. Still standing, albeit very wobbly next to the tub, she didn't have the strength to lift her leg over the edge.

"If you say 'I told you so'," she called through the crack in the door, "I will kill you."

Kyle brushed back in. "You and what army, baby?"

"One of my feet planted in your ass ought to be enough, don't you think?" she declared sweetly. She studiously ignored his rough hands on her skin as he lifted her into the tub. Her nipples didn't. They hardened into stiff little peaks and begged for those fingers. Her pussy responded in kind.

"Settled?" His voice cracked.

Ah good. She wasn't the only one affected. When he straightened, she saw his cock, hard and pressing against his fly. Aislinn smiled and melted into the heavenly hot water.

"I think so," she purred just to egg him on.

"Payback will be a bitch, you know that, right?"

"Mmm." She didn't care. At this moment in time all of her attention was held captive by the jets of water cascading over sore muscles.

"I'm coming back in twenty minutes whether you're ready or not," he grumbled.

She nodded and scooted further under until the water reached her chin, and closed her eyes.

ଓଃ

She was sound asleep when he gave up waiting for her to come out. Surprised she hadn't slipped under and drowned, Kyle knelt next to the tub, crossed his arms and propped his chin on his forearm.

"Your twenty minutes are up," he said softly.

Aislinn's scream came out more like a wobbly squawk, thanks to the chafing of her throat. Her body jerked, sloshing water over the edge and soaking him in the process.

"Jesus, Kyle, you scared the crap out of me," she sputtered. Water ran in rivulets down her chest and over her hardened nipples, drawing his attention as if she had a strobe light there.

Placing the pad of his finger against the deep mauve-colored flesh, he caught a drip. She gasped and her gaze flew to where he took the tip between his thumb and forefinger.

"I'm going to taste these sweet nipples, baby. Suck them into my mouth as far as they'll go until they're hard as rocks." He tugged it. "Stay," he commanded when she leaned forward following his pull.

Aislinn arched her back and held still when he repeated the action, stretching her breast. He released the soft tissue and lifted the slight weight in his palm. "You are perfect." He swooped in and placed a chaste kiss on first one then the other. Her chest vibrated with her low moan.

He had to taste more of her. Kyle patted the edge of the tub. "Time to get out."

"What?"

Smiling at the squeak, he repeated himself and jerked his thumbs up in the air. "Up." He reached in and started lifting her beneath her arms.

"Kyle, I..."

"Aislinn?"

Big eyes peered back at him, not with fear, but a mixture of trepidation and excitement. Her nostrils flared and the tip of her little pink tongue darted out a second before she caught her bottom lip again.

Raising an eyebrow, he asked, "What'd I say about biting on this?" He kissed her with tender lips. "Now, up."

Taking a deep breath, she rose slowly with his help,

revealing every glorious bit of skin to him, inch by agonizing inch. Her hands instinctively reached to cover her pussy.

"Uh-uh. Mine," he scolded, taking hold of both hands and guiding her to the spot he'd chosen on the rug beside the tub.

"I'm dripping everywhere, Kyle," she hissed, skin a rosy pink from the bathwater. "At least get me a towel."

"That's what the rug's for, sweetheart, and no, I don't want you covering up all this skin." Kyle took care to make sure she was comfortable before carefully spreading her thighs for his perusal.

Aislinn tried to close her legs and Kyle had a feeling she was more embarrassed than unwilling. He was about to cure her of her embarrassment really quickly.

Kyle trapped her knees with his hands. "Leave them, Aislinn, or I swear I will spank your fine ass, shitty night or not. Just feel."

Her chest rose and fell in rapid succession. Starting at one knee, he kissed and licked, nibbled and sucked his way up her thigh, getting close but skipping over the heat of her to do the same to the other leg. She whimpered and her fingernails dug into his shoulders.

Kyle worked his way back across, this time giving her what she silently demanded. Her breathy groan along with the tightening of her inner thighs was his reward. She was in no way immune to him.

With his thumbs he parted the lips of her sex, baring the tight entrance oozing with her juices. Time to feast. He licked from the bottom of her slit to the top, scooping up the cream along the way. His tongue flicked over the tiny bundle of nerves still hidden beneath its hood. Aislinn tensed again.

Where were the sexy noises he wanted to hear? He looked up at her face. Tilted back in obvious pleasure, she had a hold of that lip again with those teeth.

He'd be goddamned if she thought she needed to be silent with him. He pulled back the skin covering her clit, wrapped his lips around her sweet spot and sucked. She bucked against his mouth, but otherwise remained mute.

Using his forefinger, he slipped through her folds and swirled his tongue over the nub, continuing his assault. He penetrated slowly into her with a finger, easing his way, feeling her stretch around his digit and wishing like hell it was his cock. Tight as hell, her sheath squeezed his finger, gripping him and drawing him deeper.

Using the flat of his tongue, Kyle swept down to meet his finger, lapping at everything she poured out for him. Her breath came in shallow pants, and by now his shoulders had permanent marks from her nails. No sound.

One finger became two when he thought she was ready for more, and he pumped them in and out. A tiny moan, an insight into her contentment, slipped from her lips. He reached up and thumbed a nipple, adding another sensation. A third finger joined the first two. Her cream coated his hand, slid down his palm, filled his tongue. He could drown on her essence.

Aislinn grunted and threw a hand behind her head. He was getting close.

The tip of his tongue flicked at her swollen clit and she squeaked louder this time. He let go of her breast and focused on the nerve-rich point. With two fingers he pulled back the hood and relentlessly tongued it.

"Oh, God," she cried. "Kyle."

That's what he wanted.

Increasing the pace of his thrusting fingers, he finished her off, sucking on her clit and curving his finger inside to reach her G-spot. Unable to keep it in any longer, she screamed. Her legs went rigid, clasping his body between them, and her toes pointed. Kyle continued stroking her pussy, bringing her down from the high, lapping up every bit of release until her thighs went boneless beside him.

He massaged her legs from hip to toes. She giggled when he touched the soles of her feet. Finally she looked at him, her face glowing with satiation. It quickly turned to questioning. He knew what was coming. He could read it in her expression.

She wondered if she was supposed to reciprocate now. Kyle wanted to smash David's face into a pile of shit for creating this kind of insecurity in her.

"Bed," Kyle whispered, and then cringed when her eyes practically bugged out. He hadn't meant for that to sound like he wanted more from her right this second. "You need to sleep some more," he reassured her.

She sagged in relief. Before he could stand to help her up, she reached out and cupped his cheek.

"Thank you, Kyle."

"Mmm." He licked his lips. "Thank you. Best dessert I've ever had."

He got her dried off and settled back in his bed in ten minutes. "How's the belly, sweetheart?"

She sighed and snuggled in. "Much better, thanks to you."

Damn. If he didn't have so much to do to get ready for the party tonight, he'd join her. Spoon his way around her body and hold her in her sleep.

"I didn't do anything."

"You did." She yawned.

"Get some sleep, Aislinn, and don't worry about tonight. I've got everything under control."

"Oh my God, Kyle! I totally forgot about the party."

Sweeping her legs over the edge, she tried to stand.

"Whoa, uh-uh, sweetcheeks. Back in bed. You're not doing anything. I told you I have everything taken care of. Sleep so you can join us. Please," he added when she looked ready to run out the door and start pitching one of the massive tents outside.

She looked at him again, still unsure. "You promise you'll come get me if you need me?"

"Absolutely," he lied, settling her a second time. There wasn't anything left for her to do and he wanted her to be awake for the party. Mostly because he wanted her within sight rather than dead asleep in his bed where he couldn't keep an eye on her all the time. If David *had* found her again, this was an opportunity he might not pass up to try and get to her. A big crowd of people and lots of distractions.

He'd run into a lot of security if he thought he could try something tonight though. Plainclothes guards would be milling about and each of them would have a picture of David in hand. He'd done what he could to ensure the man couldn't crash the party but he wasn't God. Demented people had their own life plans and if David's included showing up here, Kyle would just have to be ready for him.

"Okay," she relented.

She was asleep before he closed the door.

Chapter Seven

"Aislinn? Hey, yoohoo."

Aislinn whipped her gaze to Chris. The fireworks had ended several minutes ago and the party was starting to disperse.

"Damn, girl, why am I always saying that to you?" Chris laughed. "You're always off in your own little world."

Fantastic. Caught staring into the flames of the huge bonfire Kyle had created as a centerpiece for the party. Aislinn released the death grip she had on the lawn chair's armrests and swallowed back the repeat vision she'd had of Kyle. It hadn't helped. Hadn't given her any more information. She still didn't know whose kitchen he was in or when it would happen. Hell she couldn't even see the attacker's face. What kind of clairvoyant was she?

"I heard what happened last night, Ais. Are you okay?"

"Yeah. I'm fine, now," she murmured. Well rested too, since Kyle hadn't let her out of bed until about an hour before the guests started arriving. So far no one had questioned her being the first one present.

"Why should they?" Kyle had asked her. "You're my PA. In every way now," he'd said huskily, kissing her breath away. She'd wanted to drag him into the bed she'd spent all day in and devour him like he'd devoured her next to the tub.

"Sheesh. Scary shit. You should have called me," Chris said.

"Oh, well, I—"

"Oowee. Would you look who just showed up. I swear that man could melt butter on those abs. Damn. Any time he wants to come sans shirt to work, I certainly won't complain." Chris whistled softly.

Why the hell was he naked from the waist up? He sure hadn't been like that when the party had started a few hours ago. A sudden burst of jealousy shot through Aislinn and she tamped it down. Chris wasn't interested in Kyle. In fact... Yep, there they were. TJ and Jonathan were both within hearing distance. And both were glaring at Chris like they wanted to haul her into the trees and make her forget all about Kyle.

Aislinn had no doubt Chris knew they were there too, which is why she was making such a big deal out of Kyle's appearance. Why the woman wouldn't just take what was being offered, Aislinn didn't know. Perhaps she had issues with men similar to Aislinn's.

She glanced up and saw the longing in Chris's eyes. The desire was there, but something most definitely held her back.

"He is sex on two feet, doncha think?" Chris blurted.

Aislinn nearly choked. Couldn't be more obvious, could she? "The man is your boss, Chris. You see him every day." *Plus, he's mine*, she wanted to snarl, but knew Chris's aim wasn't Kyle.

"Who cares? Oh, good, his groupies are here too," she said, acting as if she'd just noticed them.

Aislinn chuckled.

"So what are you doing for your birthday tomorrow? The big three-oh, huh?" Chris planted herself on the ground next to

Aislinn's chair and dug into the plate of food she'd carried over.

Aislinn's stomach turned. Whether it was the sight of food making her queasy or the thought that Kyle's demise still loomed in his future, she didn't know.

Trying to play cool, she shrugged. "Nothing." There wasn't anyone around to celebrate with except Kyle, and a birthday party wasn't what she had in mind with him. She groaned and crossed her legs as her pussy throbbed in remembrance of the orgasm he'd brought her to.

"I bet you had a blast as a kid with your birthday on the Fourth of July. You must have had some awesome parties. Lots of fireworks and food and all that shit," Chris mumbled around a hot wing.

Aislinn lifted a shoulder again. "It's my mom's birthday too. We sort of shared our party."

"Really?"

"Uh-huh. My grandmother's too." Aislinn stared through the bonfire at Kyle who'd taken a seat opposite her, next to one of his managers. No doubt so he could keep an eye on her like he'd warned. Somewhere in this crowd of people were other security officers waiting for something to happen.

David wouldn't show his face here though, she knew. Despite his treatment and stalking of her, the man was a coward in front of others.

She watched Kyle speak over his shoulder to TJ and laugh at whatever his friend said back.

"No shit? How'd that happen?" Chris asked.

Aislinn scrambled to remember what they'd been talking about before her mind had wandered. Oh, yeah, birthdays. *Some kind of freaky quirk of the time-space continuum, probably,* she wanted to say.

"Don't know."

In reality, Aislinn and her female ancestors *were* some kind of freaks. In her family, if you were the first daughter of a first daughter, you were born on Independence Day. You were also blessed with unruly red hair, moss green eyes—and a gift, as her mother called it—to see the future. How the traits had been passed through the females no one knew, since science had already proven it was the male who determined the sex of children. So far no males had ever been born into her family. Maybe Kyle could change...

No! Good Lord, what was she thinking?

She returned her gaze to him. He had one hand suspended in midair, supported by his elbow on the armrest. His thumb and forefinger idly rubbed together, an action she'd seen him do numerous times. Aislinn swallowed back a groan. Her nipples tightened beneath the T-shirt she'd found at the foot of his bed when she'd woken. Sweat trickled between her breasts and down the small of her back. Ack. She hated being hot and sticky. The man across from her might be able to break her of that particular discomfort in bed—she gasped at the direction of her thoughts and swiped at her hot cheeks with her hands. The back of her neck tingled and she realized she'd been staring at Kyle all this time.

He returned her heated look with one of his own, as if he knew what she was thinking about.

A log shifted, crackling in the fire and drawing her attention, breaking the connection between them.

"So, do you really think TJ and Jonathan share women?"

"What?" Aislinn laughed out loud. "Where did that come from?"

"Well, I'm just saying, you know, after what you said yesterday."

Yesterday? Sheesh, she couldn't remember this morning, let alone yesterday. "You'll have to enlighten me, Chris, my mind's a little cloudy from puking so much," she groaned, covering her stomach with her hand.

"You know, about them being in cahoots."

"I was kidding, Chris." Was she? Hadn't Kyle mentioned something about his buddies? Had she discounted whispered rumors because she couldn't imagine having sex with two men?

"Oh."

"Well don't sound so deflated, Chris."

"I'm not deflated," she screeched.

Aislinn snorted. "Now you're offended."

"Not."

Aislinn turned in her chair and faced the only true friend she'd allowed herself to have since going on the run. "You want them both," she claimed.

She had her answer in the way Chris's cheeks turned pink. "I do n-not," she stuttered.

"You're a liar."

"Oh my God, do you think this makes me a sex fiend or something?"

"No."

"Don't you dare say a word to them," Chris begged.

"Me? What would I say to them?"

"I don't know, but—"

An evil cackle filled the air and they both turned toward it. A man in a gorilla costume—must have been hotter than hell inside all that fur—ran after two small boys, alternately waving his arms and beating his chest. The kids screamed in delight as they scrambled away.

A heartbeat later one of them tripped, which sent him sprawling toward the bonfire. Chris gasped and grabbed hold of Aislinn's forearm. They watched Kyle lunge from his seat and wrap his arms around the boy. Their combined momentum took them too close to the fire. Kyle's elbow clipped the outer edge of the pyramid of stacked wood. He rolled, shielding the child with his bigger body, and came to a stop not three feet from the collapsing fire.

Ash and hot sparks spit into the dark night, landing on and around the bare skin of Kyle's back and legs. A woman screamed, then sobbed, her frantic voice muffled by the hand she held over her mouth.

Aislinn was frozen in place. People rushed around her, aiding in stamping out the small fires igniting in the dry grassy patches surrounding them, and helping Kyle to his feet. He cradled the crying boy against his chest and tucked his head under his chin. With a big hand, Kyle soothed the boy by rubbing circles on his back.

Fighting to catch her breath, Aislinn willed her heartbeat back to normal and wondered if her vision had somehow been all wrong. Maybe this is the struggle she'd seen. She quickly shook off the notion. Her dreams had never been wrong before, they wouldn't be wrong this time.

Deep inside, Aislinn had a strong suspicion the night wasn't over yet. Kyle still had another battle to overcome.

Kyle handed the shaking-like-a-leaf boy over to his mother, Turner Industries' human resource manager.

"Thank you, Mr. Turner, thank you so much," she sobbed, swiping at the twin tracks of tears running down her cheeks.

"You're welcome, Barb. I think he's fine, just shook up a bit." He ruffled the kid's hair.

A tingly ache spread across his back. He knew he'd been burned. Not bad enough to need a doctor, but a couple of spots might blister. It needed to be cleaned. And he needed to find out who the monkey was. He hadn't hired entertainment involving gorilla costumes and he sure hoped some fun-loving dad hadn't been stupidly chasing kids around a massive fire. Kyle turned in a circle but monkey man had disappeared.

Searching the crowd for Aislinn, Kyle signaled one of the security team who was helping put out tiny fires. He'd had one eye on her the entire night, making sure for one, she stayed where he'd put her, and two, that her ex didn't show his weaselly face.

"Locate the furbutt and find out who the hell he is," he told the guard.

"Yes, sir."

The ass hadn't necessarily caused the kid to trip but he'd unknowingly given David the perfect opportunity to make an appearance. It would have been easy for him to slip past the guards with all of them focused on the main event. Unless David was the furb—

Fuck! Kyle swung around, only releasing an anxious breath when he saw Aislinn walking toward him. There wasn't anyone around he didn't recognize but there was also no brown fur in sight. He waited until Aislinn was within reach before turning back to the boy. "If he needs a doctor, give me the bill, Barb."

"Oh no, Mr. Turner. I couldn't do that. I think he's fine, just a few scrapes."

Kyle nodded. "Do you have any idea who the gorilla was?"

"No, sir." She shook her head and carried her son away.

"Mr. Turner, fabulous catch. You saved his life." Joe Archer, one of his computer experts, stepped up and slapped Kyle on the back, unaware of the burns.

Kyle gritted his teeth against the flare of pain and took the good-natured pat on the back with stoic resolve. Aislinn did not.

"Stupid moron, can't you see he's hurt?" she hissed.

"Sorry, Mr. Turner." Joe hung his head, his face red with embarrassment.

"It's fine, Joe. Go, enjoy the party."

"If you're sure," Joe confirmed, looking more and more contrite.

Kyle turned and faced Aislinn. "I knew you cared," he murmured sensually.

She glared at him and curled her hands into fists. "I'll show you care."

He smiled. "You plan on using those?"

"You really want to find out?"

"Not right now, swee...air to God, my back is killing me," he dodged. Shit. He'd almost called her sweetheart in front of his entire staff. Wouldn't that go over well? He didn't give a shit how many people knew, but Aislinn would. He grasped her elbow and tugged her along. "If you'll excuse us, I'm going to steal my PA and have her look at the damage."

"Nice recovery, stud," she mumbled under her breath.

"Stud, huh? I think I like you calling me stud."

Aislinn snorted. "Don't get any ideas."

"Christ, Kyle, you're fried crispy." TJ joined them on their march up the hill.

"Oh my God, are you okay, Mr. Turner? Can I help with anything?" Chris practically ran alongside to keep up too. They were attracting people like flies.

The way Chris was already out of breath made him realize Aislinn had to jog too. He slowed his strides for the ladies.

"I know what you can help with," TJ's baritone voice growled.

"Eew. Do you mind, Mr. McFee?" Chris snapped.

Kyle noticed Aislinn purse her lips, trying to hold back a smile.

"Oh, I mind all right," TJ interjected smoothly. "I mind a whole lot." He moved closer to Chris, trapping her between himself and Aislinn.

It was the first time Kyle had seen TJ or Jon make a move on the woman he knew they both wanted. They'd been biding their time, waiting for the right moment to introduce her to their lifestyle of sharing a woman. Apparently they were done waiting.

"Move over, brute," Chris grunted, shoving TJ in the ribs with an elbow.

"Children," Aislinn chided as they walked along, "I believe there are more important things to do right now. Like clean your boss's burns."

"Boss?" Kyle and TJ echoed.

TJ pretended to choke. "Boss? Never has been, never will be. Doesn't look like he's Aislinn's boss anymore either."

"What?" Chris stammered. "Are you leaving Turner, Ais? Please, please tell me you're not leaving. I can't go back there without anyone to talk to," she gritted out, her gaze cutting to TJ.

"You can talk to me, doll," TJ crowed.

She elbowed him again, hard enough the big ex-Special Forces team leader doubled over with an oof.

"I'm not your doll, Neanderthal."

"Yet," TJ croaked.

"Never," she retorted.

"Mark my words, brown eyes, you will be." When he raised from his bent-at-the-waist position, his eyes glowed with heat and promise. There was no way Christina missed it.

"Good Lord, I feel like I'm back in high school." Aislinn shook her head and looped her arm through Kyle's. "Let's leave the lovers to quarrel on their own and put some cream on these burns, shall we?"

Chris gasped. "We are *not* lovers, Aislinn Campbell." She practically stamped her feet and Kyle had to smile.

You will be soon, he thought. Jonathan met them as they hit the door. He pulled Kyle aside and spoke in a low voice so no one else would hear. "Couldn't find anything out about Gorilla Guy, Kyle. I've got people questioning witnesses but no one seems to know anything. Teej and I are gonna stay on the property tonight. We're two minutes if you need anything."

Kyle nodded. His buddies wouldn't let him down and he welcomed the extra protection. Especially when he might get a tad preoccupied in just a little while.

Jonathan sucked in an exaggerated breath to dispel their conversation. "Jesus, Kyle, didn't we teach you anything on the team? Like maybe how to roll?"

"I did roll. If I hadn't, it'd be my face Aislinn's about to cream up right now, not my back."

"Hot damn. It isn't every day you get to tell a pretty lady to cream up your face."

"Jon, for you, it probably is every day."

The man's grin said it all. He and TJ were rumored to have pleasured at least one woman into unconsciousness. There was no doubt in Kyle's mind that both his friends' faces got creamed more than most men.

"I am so glad you guys don't talk like this at the office,"

Aislinn mumbled.

She was turned on. Kyle's cock came to life, hardening and pressing uncomfortably against his zipper. If anything could take his mind off the throbbing of his back it would be picturing Aislinn's pussy lips hugging his cock, holding on for dear life as he thrust between her legs.

He moved closer and whispered in her ear. "Why? Would it make you want me more, Aislinn?" Kyle wanted to rub his hands together. But first he had to get the burns cleaned up.

Then he'd make love to her.

He was through waiting for his woman too.

Chapter Eight

Aislinn followed Kyle into the stunning two-story log cabin—who was she kidding, the place was a freaking log mansion, for crying out loud—and cringed at the angry red marks marring the tanned skin of his back and shoulders. The embers had done a number on him. Thankfully it didn't look as bad as it could have. Maybe a blister here or there.

Replaying the scene in her head, she shivered.

The least little bit more momentum and they would have landed smack dab in the middle of the fire. If he'd been one second later, the same result. She wondered if what she'd seen tonight paled in comparison to some of the things he'd done as a SEAL. Had it seemed like child's play to him, being a hero? Did he see himself the same way?

They moved through the mudroom where Kyle gingerly leaned against the washing machine and kicked off his shoes before trudging on. She hadn't had much time earlier to see the monstrosity of his house. Most of the day she'd been asleep, and the rest of the time she'd been ordered to stay in bed.

After the notorious bath, the one time she'd gotten up to use the toilet Kyle had barged in looking ready to swat her butt as if she were a kid who'd broken a neighbor's window. Not even her argument that she'd had to go to the bathroom had eased his demeanor.

"When I didn't see you in bed, I thought something had happened to you," he'd barked, breathing heavily.

It should have pissed her off. How many times had David treated her like an object he owned? She was over being treated like dirt.

But something about the wild look in Kyle's eyes told her his hysteria was different. Laced with actual fear, not anger. Kyle had been *afraid* something had happened to her. He'd said so, it had just taken a few seconds to realize she wasn't still in the past and that he hadn't been angry with her for defying his order.

Instead he'd requested. He'd *asked* her to stay in bed for the day so she wouldn't be too tired to attend the party. And her heart had melted over his concern for her wellbeing. She probably would have stayed curled up under his covers anyway, since even now she didn't fully trust her tummy not to start revolting again.

Aislinn barely glanced through the doorway to the kitchen when they passed it on their right. What she did glimpse was an oversized stainless-steel fridge and a center island complete with hanging copper pots and pans any chef would swoon to be near.

For someone who said they didn't cook, Kyle sure had a dream kitchen. She wouldn't mind moving around in there herself for a minute or two.

She came to a jerking halt three feet past the door and swallowed around the lump in her throat.

"Where's your med box, Kyle?" Jonathan's question flowed around her, buzzing in her ears, and the floor threatened to rise up and slap her. She swayed, brushing the wall with her shoulder.

One hand on his hip, Kyle arched his back and winced. "In

the hall closet. Top shelf."

Aislinn closed her eyes and put her hand on the wall to keep from falling. She massaged her temples trying to relieve the pounding taking up residence in her head.

"Aislinn?"

Kyle's voice called out from far away. His hand gently gripped her forearm. What had he said? What had caused this? Something she'd seen... Bile rose in her throat. She choked it back and bolted for the bathroom. Thank God she remembered there being one off this hallway.

"Christ, baby. What the hell happened?"

Make him go away, she prayed, hanging onto the toilet seat and begging her stomach into submission.

"Nothing. I'm fine." *A liar, but fine.* At least she knew which kitchen she'd seen in her vision. His own.

"I'm good," she said more convincingly. She hoped. "Residual from last night I guess." She wasn't about to bring it up in front of Jonathan.

"Here you go." Jon returned and handed the typical white box with a red cross imprint to Kyle. "You okay, Aislinn? You look a little pale."

She nodded. Kyle didn't take his semi-narrowed gaze off her. "She's fine. More of what happened last night."

His tone said he didn't believe her for a second but would go along with her until they were alone.

"Good. I'm outta here then. Teej and I gotta get Christina home." Jon wiggled his eyebrows, dispelling the tension in the small bathroom.

Aislinn inhaled and broke the staring contest with Kyle.

"I don't think she likes you. How on Earth did you get her to let you take her home?" She laughed.

Jon feigned a wounded look. “Not like me? What’s not to like?” He lifted an arm and flexed his muscles. “Me strong,” he grunted. “Besides, she likes me.” His nostrils flared and a serious tone replaced the teasing. “She just doesn’t know it yet.”

Aislinn sobered. “I think there’s a reason she doesn’t like men, Jonathan.”

“And it’s my job to ferret out what the reason is and change her mind, ma’am.”

She wrinkled her nose at his formality. “I think you could.”

Jon nodded sharply once. “Teej and I both,” he promised.

Unsurprised by his announcement, Aislinn returned his nod. They wouldn’t hurt her. Both of them were big, tall and a bit overpowering but in the last six months she’d seen enough of the way they treated her best friend to know the worst they could do was break her heart.

She sighed. A broken heart was something both she and Chris might be handed on a silver platter with these three men involved. Kyle must have somehow sensed her turn of thoughts. He shoved Jonathan out the door.

“Get the hell out of here. I’m injured in case you hadn’t noticed.”

Jon snorted. “Right.” He winked at Aislinn over Kyle’s shoulder. “Make sure you get plenty of rest tonight then.”

Jon dodged the fist thrown in his direction and jogged off.

Aislinn cleared her throat. “Turn around.”

He spun around, catching her upper arms to keep her from falling since they were so close. “What’d you see, sweetheart? And don’t even attempt to lie to me, I’ll see through it.”

Of course he would.

“The kitchen is yours.”

“Are you sure?”

"Yes. I saw the refrigerator as we passed. It's the same one."

"All right then."

"That's it? That's all you're gonna say?" she snapped. Damn infuriating man. They should be leaving the house. Getting away from the scene of the future crime.

God. How lame did she sound?

"What do you want me to say?"

"I want you to leave, Kyle."

"Do you know when this is supposed to happen, sweetheart?"

No, damn it, which made the whole damn thing shittier.

"I didn't think so."

"I haven't said anything." She slapped the antibiotic cream on a red spot on his back. He hissed and arched. "Shit. I'm sorry, Kyle."

"It's fine."

The way he had to grind the words out between clenched teeth made it anything but fine, and made her feel like a big heel. She rubbed the cream softly around the slightly burned areas, enjoying the feel of taut, smooth skin beneath her fingertips. Muscles rippled, his breathing grew faster, and he bent over the sink, supporting himself with his hands on either side of the bowl.

"Aislinn?"

"Hmm?"

"If you don't want this to go any further, you better stop now."

Stop? Did she want to stop? She added a second hand to the first, smearing the cream and running her palms up to his shoulders. Could she do this?

"Last chance," he offered, sounding guttural. She glanced at his face in the mirror and gasped. He looked like a man starved. For her.

"That's it." Kyle spun around and faced the woman tying his dick in a knot and took hold of her face with both hands. "No more waiting." He descended on her lips, spreading them and coercing her into kissing him back. Coercion wasn't necessary.

Her arms went around his waist and she tilted her head to give him better access. Their tongues tangled. Fuck she was sweet.

Kyle turned them, lifted her onto the counter and insinuated himself between her thighs. He needed to get closer, as close as physically possible. Inside her. Now. Easing his thumbs into the waistband of her shorts, he tugged them over her hips. She helped, raising up and allowing him to remove them completely. Kyle dropped to his knees and dragged her hips forward until her pussy begged for his mouth.

Fire-red curls shielded her entrance, a testament to her natural color.

"You smell so fucking amazing." Starting at her knee, he nibbled and kissed his way to her pussy, shiny with her juices. He spread her labia with his thumbs and licked her slit, pausing at the top to swirl his tongue around her beaded clit.

Her hips shot upward, smashing her wet heat into his face. Kyle took advantage and filled her with his tongue, thrusting deep. She moaned and threaded her fingers through his hair, alternately tugging him toward her and pushing him away like she didn't know if she wanted him closer or not.

No way was he moving. Not when he was finally where he

most wanted to be. Aislinn made this tiny squeak, a subtle moan, and he knew she was biting her damn lip again. On his haunches, he retreated and stared up at her. Her head was thrown back. She caught herself after his abrupt departure by placing her hands behind her on the counter. The action pushed out her breasts. Her nipples poked through the cotton, demanding attention.

"Take the shirt off," he growled.

Aislinn lifted her head and gazed at him through lowered eyelids.

"Wha—?"

"The shirt, Aislinn, take it off."

She swallowed, crossed her arms and lifted the hem, revealing inch by beautiful inch of tummy and then breasts. With her hands high above her, her breasts rose. Kyle reached for a nipple while she was caught up in the fabric and twisted it between his fingers. Aislinn groaned and her elbows dropped, shirt still covering her head.

"Off."

She flung it across the room.

"Better." He continued manipulating the tight bud with one hand and returned his attention to her pussy. He swiped her gleaming wet slit again with his tongue. "Put your hands on the counter behind you and don't move them."

Aislinn whimpered when he sucked her clit into his mouth. She squirmed and dug her heels into the cabinet below. He could eat her all day and never get tired of it.

Switching to the other nipple, he gave it some love too, pinching and rolling until her hands came forward to grip his forearm. Long nails dug into his skin leaving tiny crescent marks. Kyle stopped altogether until she looked at him again.

"Please don't stop," she begged, her eyes wide, her hips fidgeting.

"Then put your hands back, sweetheart. I love you touching me, but right now I'm too close."

Aislinn gasped and jerked her gaze to where her fingers pressed into his arm. She let go of him like he'd burned her and that sweet little lip went between her teeth.

"Uh-uh." He rubbed it with his thumb and watched the tip of her tongue dart out to capture the digit.

"Taste yourself on me, baby?"

She nodded, her face full of desire and heat.

"Fuck." Kyle stood and yanked at the button of his fly while backing up a step. The zipper rasped as he carefully tugged it down over his hard-on. His cock sprang free, thick and long. It captured Aislinn's scrutiny immediately. He gripped the length and rubbed it from root to tip with a fist, imagining it was her pussy wrapped around him.

A puff of air escaped Aislinn's lips.

"It'll fit."

Never taking her eyes off his groin, she nodded again. Kyle smiled and slowly moved between her spread thighs, placing his hands at her waist. His cock bobbed against her outer lips. Aislinn laid her forehead against his chest.

"I know it will," she whispered.

Damn, she would kill him for sure. He slid his hands up her sides and lifted the weight of her breasts. Soft and small and perfect. He flicked at the nubs with his thumbs, drawing them into tighter points.

His cock head shifted amongst her slippery folds, finding its way inside. Grinding his teeth together, Kyle slammed his eyes shut and fought not to start pounding into her sheath. It would be so easy.

"Fuck me, Kyle."

Three little words.

Three little words that shattered his sanity. He gripped her hips and thrust to the hilt, mindless of the fact he hadn't donned protection. Nothing would tear him away from her. Especially now, when he felt every one of her inner muscles clinging to his cock, dragging him deeper.

She clung to him with her legs, grasping his waist by hooking her heels at the small of his back. The movement sucked him closer. Not even a millimeter separated them.

He gave what she wanted, withdrawing and slamming back into her, and captured her cries in his mouth.

"God, Aislinn." He palmed her ass and held her still for his thrusts. Sweat helped her glide on the marble top. Her grunts filled the small space, mingling with his. She lifted her hands, placing them on his shoulders.

Kyle hissed at the contact of her touch on his burns. He couldn't care less. She could touch him anytime she wanted to.

"Shit," she cried.

"No. Leave 'em. Hold on to me." He slipped his thumb between them and circled her clit. The tension built in her pussy and the inner walls contracted on him.

He slammed home with a shout and came inside her. Her cries echoed his and every vibration in her pussy wrung another surge from his cock.

Breathing heavily, Kyle hugged the woman he wanted to spend the rest of his life with. He wiped the sweaty hair from her neck and nuzzled the column of her throat, laving it with kisses and love bites.

"Oh my God," she whispered, shivering with the cool air on

her heated skin.

He needed more. Still embedded deep in her vagina, Kyle scooped her up and carried her to his first-floor bedroom.

"Let's do it again," he growled in her ear.

A tiny part of her brain screamed, "Nooooo." The vast majority said, "Yes, yes, yes." Kyle had shown her how wonderful sex could be. It wasn't supposed to be painful, but a meshing of flesh and souls and pleasure. And suddenly she found herself wanting more instead of cringing at the mere thought.

Something about the way Kyle touched her and moved in her made their joining special. Did he see it the same way? Was she simply another conquest for him? Her feet hit the mattress a second before her butt did. The action pulled his cock free and for the first time she got a good look at one aspect of the male body she'd thought was meant for pain.

She'd glimpsed it for a few seconds when he'd first freed himself. An instant flare of panic had surged to the surface when she'd seen the size of it. It was bigger than David's in both circumference and length and should have cut her in two. Kyle had guessed her anxiety and settled her with two words. "It'll fit."

Boy had it. Aislinn squirmed on his comforter, crazily thinking about the wet spot she was surely leaving on its surface. She licked her lips as his penis bobbed before her and found herself wanting to reach out and touch. She saw it in a whole new light. Such a contrast of textures. Soft and velvet skin over steel. The purpled head wept a drop of come from its slit. Would it taste different from her previous experiences?

"Touch if you want, sweetheart."

Aislinn sucked in a breath. "How did you…?"

"It's written all over your face." He palmed her cheek and smoothed his thumb over her skin. The tender caress was nearly her undoing. What had she done to deserve this man?

Because you've already been through hell.

"My body is yours to play with."

Could she?

"Yes."

"Stop reading my mind, damn it." She couldn't help but smile.

Kyle laughed. "It's easy to do when you're broadcasting with every wanting look you give me." He grasped her hand and giving her time to pull away, slowly guided it to his cock.

Aislinn wrapped her fingers around the base, marveling at how her fingertips and thumb didn't meet. She had cradled this in her body and wanted to again. Now.

She glanced up at him, expecting to see a grin of domination on his face. What she saw stopped her heart. His eyes were closed, his nostrils flared, and he appeared to be having trouble breathing. She pumped him once and marveled at the tiny jump of muscle along his jaw.

Twice more she moved her gripped fist on his shaft. Kyle snagged her wrist on the third pass.

"I can't take any more."

Not, "Harder, Aisly, you know how I like it." No pulling her hair until tears ran down her cheeks and barking at her to, "Take me in your mouth."

"I want to be inside you when I come," Kyle groaned.

Oh God. She wanted to cry. She wanted to laugh. She wanted Kyle inside her.

"Please," she whispered and moved to lie back.

He stopped her. "No." After crawling onto the bed, Kyle stretched out on his back, like he'd never been burned, his hands folded beneath his head, his feet spread about a foot apart. Standing at a proud full mast, his cock begged for her. "You're in charge, baby. Do whatever you want."

She did cry then, as she straddled his thighs. Her pussy grazed the head of his penis, making it jump in anticipation. She had her own fair share of that.

Kyle's eyes glittered and his muscles bunched along his chest and abdomen. Aislinn trailed her fingertips over his tan, sweat-slicked skin.

"I'm not sure what to do," she admitted.

He smiled. "Whatever you do turns me on so don't worry about making it good for me. Do what you like."

"But I—"

He shushed her with a finger over her lips. "Do what feels good, Aislinn."

Her gaze wandered over his upper body from his eyes to the point where her mound rubbed against the tip of his erection. She must have subconsciously sunk lower. Shifting her hips, she nudged her clit against him. Tiny sparks shot through the raw bundle of nerves. It felt fantastic. She closed her eyes and did it again. And again.

Still blind, she took his cock in hand and slid it between her labia, moaning at the sensation.

"Aislinn. Honey." Kyle panted below her. "Unh."

She opened her eyes to see his head thrown back. His hips lifted, pressing his cock into her sheath, while he dug his heels into the mattress. She lowered herself onto his cock, wincing a tiny bit at the stretching of abused muscles from their countertop session.

Kyle hissed as she rose and fell in a lazy rhythm. “Remind me never to give you control again,” he ground out.

She purred. Aislinn Campbell purred and sank all the way down, impaling herself on him. She rolled her hips, dragging her clit on the thick hair covering his groin. Her belly tingled, her nipples throbbed. With her finger and thumb, she alternately pinched them, tugging on them until they hardened. The other hand went to her clit, slippery with their combined juices.

“Ride me, Aislinn. Please.”

An exhilarating thrill flowed through her. For the first time in her life she had made a man beg.

Up, down, up, down. She was so close. Kyle’s thighs bunched beneath her, yet his hands remained behind his head. His iron control looked shaky but he held onto it somehow.

The pressure built, swelling her clit. She tapped it with one finger and exploded, screaming out her pleasure.

Kyle’s hands gripped her hips while her orgasm continued to roll through her. He pistoned his cock inside her, reaching a depth she hadn’t accomplished on her own. Three, four, five strokes and he embedded himself deep inside her and shouted his own release. She felt every spurt of his come splashing her womb.

Later—she had no idea how long—his fingers loosened on her skin and she fell forward, tucking her head beneath his chin. His lungs heaved the same as hers. Their hearts pounded together. Kyle wrapped his arms around her and held her tight, his cock still buried in her pussy.

She fell asleep hugged close to his body and surrounded by his protection.

Chapter Nine

Aislinn sighed and tried to roll over. Kyle's arm draped across her belly held her captive, but he'd be sorry if she didn't get out soon. She wiggled, doing her best not to wake him, and cringed as the movement jarred seldom-used, sore muscles.

Insatiable man. She couldn't even remember how many times he'd made love to her. Or how many mind-blowing orgasms he'd caused her to have.

Kyle mumbled something in his sleep and his hand moved on the sheets as if searching for her. For her? Or for whatever temporary woman normally graced his bed?

Stop, she scolded herself. For some inexplicable reason, she trusted his word. Probably had a lot to do with what her mother had told her on the phone last night at the restaurant. She shivered and clutched her still sore belly at the mere thought of the place.

Kyle had also told her he hadn't been with anyone since she'd come to work at Turner Industries. Rumor had it a different woman every weekend paraded through his office. Aislinn had yet to see any evidence of this which could only mean two things—either she was really blind and the rumor was true, or Kyle had stopped seeing other women when he said he had.

Her stomach grumbled, reminding her the last time she'd eaten had been at the party. After their second round of unbelievable, wild monkey sex, he'd tried to get her to the kitchen to eat.

"Are you nuts?" she'd asked. "Or just stupid?"

Sure, she didn't have any idea when her vision would come to fruition, but no way would she purposefully offer him up on a silver platter.

He'd raised an eyebrow over one of those beautiful blue eyes and said sarcastically, "Shall I move out?"

Kyle was right, the bastard. Running from the problem wouldn't alter the eventual outcome. And if anyone was tired of running, it was Aislinn.

She curled her hands into fists and stared through the moonlit darkness at the obstinate man. Even in sleep he presented an overbearing ex-Special Forces he-man.

But he was *her* he-man and she wasn't about to allow him to walk into a trap. If he didn't want to protect himself, she'd do it for him.

Aislinn tiptoed to the bathroom. When she was done, she stood in the bedroom doorway. Kyle's room was on the first floor, one of a few. She hadn't been upstairs and she had to wonder how many guestrooms there actually were. What the hell did a man alone need with all this house anyway? Planning for the future? He would have to have twelve kids to fill it.

She wrinkled her nose and looked down at her flat tummy. Uh-uh. Absolutely not. One, two, maybe—

What was she thinking? She gave one last glance at the man in the bed. She just wanted a minute alone.

To the right was the kitchen, to the left, the sunken living room. Which door should she choose? Her stomach begged for the former, her brain easily chose the latter. If she never saw his kitchen it would be too soon.

A flatscreen occupied one wall. The rest of the room was taken up by butter-soft leather couches and deep chairs. A typical man's choice for furniture but not completely overloaded by testosterone. Comfortable.

A creak alerted her to a second presence in the room. Smiling, Aislinn swung around, expecting to see Kyle. Panic swept through her.

"You stupid bitch." Spittle shot from her ex's mouth. He jumped at her, cutting her scream off with a thick meaty hand. His fingers squeezed her jaw hard enough she thought for sure it would snap. His other hand swung her around and yanked her back to his front.

"Every fucking time I get close to you, you disappear," he snarled in her ear. His breath smelled foul and full of alcohol.

David kicked at her feet to get her moving. His toes sent a shooting pain up her calf. She twisted in his crushing hold. Licking her ear, he hissed, "You didn't actually think I'd let you go, did you?"

Her stomach turned, threatening to spill what little contents it contained. She barely had room to suck in air through nostrils closed off by his hand. Tears sprang to her eyes. She cried out, but the noise only came out as a muffled groan.

He moved, causing her to trip forward. David pinned his arm beneath her breasts, crushing her ribs. Much longer and she'd pass out from lack of oxygen.

David dragged her down the hall. "I'll kill him for touching my cunt," he spat.

"Mmm-mmm. Mmm-mmm," she shouted. The words were drowned out behind his hand. Aislinn shook her head against him. He held fast even when she tumbled, nearly bringing both of them down.

"Did you like the gorilla get-up? Nice, huh? Hotter than fuck," he rasped, "but it did the trick. Caused a nice scene and gained me entry to the house. Where I've been the whole fucking night waiting for you to fucking leave that cocksucker's bed." David wrenched her head toward his face so sharply, her vertebrae popped. Aislinn clawed at his hand, drawing blood with her fingernails. David never flinched.

"How's your belly, baby? A tiny bit was all it took. That restaurant should be more careful who they let in. And you should have never fucking run from me. Consider this a punishment. Next time it'll be worse."

She shook from head to toe and tried to get her jaw open enough to bite the fleshy palm squeezing her face.

"Took me five and a half long fucking months to find you. A couple weeks planning time and now you're mine again. You did well this time. But not good enough. I've got you now and as soon as I stash you, I'm coming back for your little loverboy, Aisly." His tongue lapped at her cheek and she jerked. "I'm gonna cut his fucking dick off and shove it down his throat," he whispered raggedly.

She fought him like a wildcat, ignoring the pain it caused her and screaming for all she was worth. Surely Kyle's Special Forces background would kick in and her struggles would wake him. Her bare heel connected with his shin and he grunted but continued dragging her to the front door.

With two fingers she jabbed at his face.

"You fucking cunt," he howled, losing his grip.

Aislinn jerked free and stumbled away from him, choking and gasping for breath. She made it to the doorway before David snarled, "I don't think so, bitch." He stormed after her.

Their momentum carried them further down the hall. Her shoulder slammed into the doorframe of the kitchen, bringing stars to her vision.

David shoved her all the way through the door.

"Hold it right there, David."

With a roar, David reversed their positions, using Aislinn as a shield. She heard a click and from nowhere, a knife appeared in his hand.

Aislinn gasped as the cold steel bit into her flesh between two ribs.

"I will stick her like a pig if you move one more inch," he hurled.

For the first time Aislinn noticed Kyle's lack of clothes. Only a pair of boxers and the gun he held in front of him. Even mostly naked, he resonated a deadly calm with his total lack of emotion. He looked bored. Only the telltale ticking of his jaw told her he was pissed.

If she didn't do something right now, his life would end here in this kitchen, in the dead of night. The same as her vision.

She had that on her side at least. David didn't have a clue she already knew the sequence of events about to unfold. For once in her life, she was in the position to change the outcome.

"Interesting," Kyle commented in a neutral tone.

Oh God. Aislinn swallowed the fear threatening to demolish her. Kyle wasn't bored at all, he was waiting for his opportunity. It was up to her to create one and trust that whatever happened, he wouldn't get himself killed. She wouldn't let him.

Her gaze met his. A blink later, and the tiniest downward nod of his head, she knew what to do.

Aislinn dropped like a sack of potatoes. The added weight

threw David off guard. The motion should have given Kyle the space he needed. Instead, David pivoted and kicked out, connecting with Kyle's gun hand while still holding onto her. The opportunity for Kyle to fire was gone and so was his gun. She rammed two fingers over her shoulder and stabbed at David's face. She felt soft flesh but couldn't tell where she'd hit him. He screamed out and grabbed for his face.

Scrambling to her feet, she ran into Kyle's arms and buried her face against his chest.

David's scream had only been a diversion. With a guttural cry, he leaped at her and Kyle, knife high in the air. Kyle shoved Aislinn aside. She went down, smacking the back of her head on the tabletop, and had a hard time focusing as the two men grappled with each other in an obscene dance around the room. They locked onto each other's arms like wrestlers would, David still holding the knife, which glinted in the moonlight.

It suddenly clattered to the floor between their feet and David's hand broke loose from Kyle's hold. He threw a punch at Kyle's face. Flesh connected with a thud. Kyle returned the favor and blood splattered from David's mouth.

She wanted to help. She wanted to do something, but this wasn't her area of expertise, it was Kyle's. Aislinn shook her head and fought the cobwebs and the throbbing at the back of her skull.

A foot kicked the gun across the tile floor, drawing her attention. Sluggishly, she crawled to it, wincing at every grunt and groan and thump of fist on body.

She stood and cradled the foreign object in her hands like she'd seen on TV and prayed the safety was off and that she didn't hit Kyle.

A loud roar went up and Kyle flung them to the ground. They rolled, still kicking and punching. A second later David, with top advantage, held something in the air. It clicked open and moonlight glinted from the steel, exactly like it had happened in her vision.

"Look out!" Aislinn screamed. Her heart pounded in her ears, drowning everything else out.

Kyle reared up and twisted as the knife came down. It sliced into skin high up on his arm, spilling blood. With a vicious howl, Kyle took David's head in his hands and slammed it into the center island. The crack of bone and marble that followed made Aislinn go weak in the knees.

"I'll take that," a deep voice rumbled behind her.

Aislinn screamed and jumped as two strong hands descended over hers and relieved her of the gun she held in a death grip.

"Fuck, Teej," Kyle groaned, panting hard. He rolled out from beneath the unconscious David and held his shoulder. Blood oozed from between his fingers. "What the hell took you so long?"

TJ chuckled. "I was just watching, waiting to see if you needed me."

"You've been here this whole time and did nothing?" Aislinn shrieked.

Kyle dragged himself off the floor. He enveloped her in a bear hug, heedless of the blood he transferred. His hand twisted in her hair as if he'd never let her go and his lips kissed every part of her face he could get to.

"No, darlin'. Kyle pushed the panic button." TJ looked at his precision military watch. "Took me two minutes and twenty-eight seconds to get here."

Two minutes? God it seemed like they'd been fighting for hours. Two minutes?

"Police are on their way, Kyle."

He nodded over her head. "Get that fucker out of my sight."

"Will do."

Chapter Ten

Kyle tossed the butter knife from Aislinn's fingers into the sink and wrapped his arms around her. She leaned back into his chest. "Happy Fourth of July birthday, sweetheart."

Aislinn laughed. "Thank you. Why are you out of bed?" They'd gone to the hospital in the early hours of the morning and gotten Kyle's arm practically stitched back on, then she'd spent the day with him, making sure he did what he'd been told.

"Mmm." He nuzzled the back of her neck. "I'm tired of laying down, Mommy."

She laughed and slapped at his hands as he raised them to her breasts. A second later she stilled.

"He's never going to leave me alone, is he?" she murmured, staring out the kitchen window at nothing.

Wrapping her long red hair in his fist, Kyle turned her and hugged her tight. He hated seeing her like this. He should have killed the little prick. Snapped his neck instead of knocking him out.

"He can't hurt you anymore. Not behind bars where he belongs, sweetheart." Kyle would make sure the bastard never saw the light of day to bother Aislinn again.

She shook her head.

He straightened and took her face in his hands. Raising an eyebrow, he said, "You doubt me? I make the most sophisticated security equipment known to man. I employ the best agents to use that equipment. There's nothing he can do without us knowing it."

"Do you think so? He got in your house, Kyle."

Kyle's initial laugh sobered instantly. "I'm not happy about that either." He could have told her he'd be looking into what the fuck had happened, but it wouldn't change things. Security was tight but there had been about a hundred people on the grounds.

"I'm not blaming you," she said.

"I know." He blamed himself though. It had been his job to protect her. Instead he'd almost gotten her killed. He'd have to live with that the rest of his life.

He took a deep breath and kissed her forehead. Her scent washed over him, headed straight for his groin. "I want to fuck you, baby."

"No."

"Excuse me?"

"You know what the doctor said. No physical activity."

"I won't be physical."

Aislinn snorted. "Right."

"I won't," he swore, groaning when she pulled away and shook her finger at him.

"No."

"Please."

"Ahh, he's resorted to begging." She chuckled and backed slowly out of the kitchen. One foot and then the other, her hips swayed with each step, and her pebbled nipples taunted him. He followed, stalking her just as slowly.

She'd brought him breakfast in bed this morning after forcing him not to get up. Literally. She'd tied his ass to the bed with the silk tie of his robe, only letting him up to take care of nature. His nostrils flared remembering the scene.

Naked as the day he was born, he'd eaten, giving her time to think she'd won. Then he'd slipped out of his confines—he was a Special Forces team member for fuck's sake, there wasn't any situation he couldn't get out of—and hunted her down. She'd been in the kitchen, standing at the center island in only his T-shirt. Yeah, it hung almost to mid-thigh, but damn he'd never seen anything sexier.

Her butt was bare beneath the shirt too, enticing him with the smell of her pussy, begging for him to lay her out and fuck her senseless. He could do it with minimal movement on his part and if she couldn't feel the way his raging hard-on tented his boxers she was just plain mean.

"He also said you should keep me comfortable." He took another step, stalking her out the door. Wouldn't be much longer before he had her knees hitting the edge of his bed. A little push on her shoulders and she'd be eye, no, *mouth* level with what needed the most comforting right now. If his dick got any harder it might break off.

"Comfortable is lying in bed, reading a book." Her back hit the wall in the hallway and she turned to continue backpedaling, never taking her gaze off him.

She bit her lip which only fueled his hunger to have those teeth nibbling on his cock.

"Your idea of resting and mine are two different things."

"I can see that," she breathed, her glance wandering to his erection. He watched her swallow as her eyes widened.

A second later he swallowed. Her wide-eyed look transformed into a calculated narrow-eyed glare of intent. Kyle didn't know whether he liked that look or not.

The corners of her mouth turned up and he knew he was in trouble. Aislinn stopped moving and put her hands on her hips.

"Why, Mr. Turner, are you happy to see me, or is that a—"

"Don't say it," he growled. "You know damn well there is no banana in my non-existent pockets."

"Hmm." Her tongue poked out to wet her lips. "So I guess there's no reason I should fish out the piece of fruit making you so uncomfortable there, huh?"

Kyle groaned and closed his eyes. The little witch would kill him.

"Okay, here's the deal," she articulated.

He already didn't like the sound of her "deal".

She raised an eyebrow and sucked in her cheeks, further exasperating him. One more movement out of that mouth and he'd end up fucking her against the wall. He took another step until not more than a foot stood between them. She held her ground.

"If you promise..." She hesitated and he felt every thump of his heart against his breastbone.

"Oh, I promise," he whispered.

Aislinn cocked her head and gave him an annoyed look. "You don't even know what I was going to say."

"Doesn't matter."

"So if I say, if you promise to take a nap right now, I'll let you fuck me *tonight*, you'll go along with it."

Kyle hung his head, lamenting her shitty deal.

"Thought so."

"It's not nice to tease your boss."

"And that, dear Kyle, is your problem. You're not my boss

right now, you're my lover."

"Mmm." He snuck closer and gripped her waist with both hands, ignoring the twinge in his upper arm. "I do like the sound of lover on your lips." He leaned back at the waist so he could see her face. "Now give me a better deal."

She deflated on a sigh, placing her hands on his chest and patting him. "Fine. If you promise to stay absolutely still I will..." The rest of her sentence trailed off.

"What? What was the rest of that?" He bent at the knees and lifted her chin with a thumb. "You were mumbling, sweetheart."

She cleared her throat. "I said, if you promise to stay very still I will...kiss you."

"I can kiss you anytime I want, Aislinn." Kyle proved it by settling his mouth on hers and catching her gasp. She sagged against him and threaded her arms beneath his and around him.

"See?" he breathed, sweeping his lips across her cheek and up to her ear, where he sucked the lobe into his mouth. "Where exactly are you going to kiss me that I'd have to work on keeping still?"

"Ugh." Aislinn tilted her head and he took advantage of her bared neck and throat. "You're going to make me say it, aren't you?"

"Absolutely."

"Then I guess you don't get anything." Her blush deepened.

"Then I guess I can fuck you right here on this wall." Kyle grabbed the hem of her shirt. He slid it up and over her hips before cupping the cheeks of her ass and lifting her.

Aislinn shrieked and heedful of his bad arm slapped at his chest and other arm. "Put me down, Kyle Turner."

"No." Fuck what the doctor had said. He needed her.

"Fine," she yelled, her body tense. "I'll give you a blow job. Are you satisfied?"

"Not yet. But I will be as soon as you give me that...kiss," he mocked. He marched her, still backward, into the bedroom, only stopping when they reached the bed. Every step he punctuated with a kiss. When they could go no further, he slipped his hands beneath the shirt and covered her breasts. He pinched her nipples for a brief moment before yanking the shirt over her head.

"I want to see you." His chest rumbled when he spoke.

"And now you can." She reversed their positions and pushed at his chest until he sat on the edge of the bed. "Oops," she giggled. "Forgot these." Aislinn tugged at the waistband of his boxers.

He obliged, lifting his hips to help her strip them off. His cock jutted out, the slit seeping with pre-come. Aislinn's tiny hand wrapped around its circumference at the base and he nearly jumped out of his skin. She didn't say a word as her lips descended. The head of his cock disappeared and she sucked him like a lollipop.

Holy fuck, his eyes rolled back and his elbows gave out. She took him deeper, swallowing half his cock.

Kyle watched her take him in. The rubbery tip tentatively touched the back of her throat. For a second she gagged and retreated. Her tongue tasted him, lapping along the vein underneath and flicking at the broad head. Kyle's balls drew up tight and he felt ready to explode and fill her hot mouth with his come.

Red curls sifted across his thighs, adding to the sensations already seizing his entire body. Her head bobbed up and down, drawing on his cock, literally sucking the come from his balls.

Kyle inhaled sharply.

"Sweetheart," he ground out, trying to lift her head off him, "I'm going to come." He was surprised at the croak in his voice.

"I know," she hummed.

His toes curled into the carpet and if his thigh muscles got any tighter, they'd likely snap.

"Then finish it," he snarled, twisting his fist in her hair. She smiled. It was a devil's smile.

"Mmm." Her lips closed over him again, and her hand joined her mouth in working his cock.

Throwing his head back, Kyle shouted with his release. Long hot spurts shot from his cock and Aislinn swallowed him over and over, milking him.

When he was finally wrung dry, he collapsed back on the bed. He hardly felt the sting of the burns on his back, but a sharp pain singed his arm. He winced but otherwise ignored the flash. Aislinn crawled onto the bed beside him and straddled his body. If he hadn't just had an explosive orgasm, leaving him drained and fighting for a breath, he could have slipped inside her and gone again.

One thing was for sure, their sex life wouldn't be boring.

He felt like lead. Couldn't even lift his hand to wipe the hair falling over her eyes away. She smiled down at him and purred with contentment.

"Ready for a nap now?"

Nap? "No fucking way, baby." Kyle forced his eyelids open and fought his way across the bed so his feet were no longer dangling off. In a minute he'd have her under him, thighs spread so he could taste her the way she had him.

She chuckled. "Is that why you can't keep your eyes open?"

"They are." Were they? "I think you drained me."

“And you were so still for me,” she teased.

“I’ll be still for you any time,” he mumbled. Maybe she was right. Maybe he did need a tiny little rest. Hell, he’d slept in some of the worst situations on the planet with one eye and ear open. He could do it again.

“I love you, Kyle Turner III.”

He thought his hand went to her waist and pulled her closer. At least, he thought he felt her weight sink onto his good side, wrapping him in her heat.

No way would he let her get away with thinking he hadn’t heard her though.

He kissed her forehead and murmured, “I love you too, Aislinn Campbell. Forever.”

The Strength of Three

Dedication

Thanks Nic and TK for your input. And, sis, I love the couch. I think I'll keep it. ☺

Chapter One

Soft rock blared from a pair of onstage speakers. Christina Marshall rubbed at her temple, trying to ease the growing ache. She could win an Oscar for tonight's outstanding performance. No one had noticed her underlying unease. At least, she didn't think anyone had.

She glanced around the rented reception room again. As parties went for landing a monstrous account, this one beat all, Chris guessed, since she wasn't into this kind of thing. Her coworkers danced and talked and seemed to truly be having a good time. All while drowning themselves in whatever they could purchase from the cash bar. One big Friday after-work happy hour.

Christina had to admit that everyone did *appear* happy. Except for her. *No! You do look happy, Marshall. Suck it up. One hour. You only have to make it one hour before slipping out.* That was the time she'd set for herself and she was going to stick to it even if it killed her. Chris slapped a goofy smile on her face and hoped it didn't make her look like she needed a straitjacket.

Yep, she was most definitely happy. Happy as a clam. Happy as a lark.

Right. She would be just as happy to have a huge, hairy wart suddenly show up on her nose tomorrow morning.

Maybe clenching her glass full of now-warm Coke hard enough to shatter it constituted happiness. Or grinding her teeth and jaw into oblivion. Nope, had to be the sharp pain settling smack dab between her eyes because she couldn't stop darting her attention from one coworker to the next, making sure they didn't bring their drunken, happy asses any closer to her.

Happy.

Her best friend, Aislinn, now fiancée to their boss, Kyle Turner III, sauntered over. "Your smile's fading, sweetie. You're supposed to at least *look* like you're having fun."

"I am having fun." *A regular ol' barrel of monkeys.*

"Right. That's why you're coming across like someone killed your puppy." Aislinn sipped her ice tea, a drink Chris knew her friend had chosen in deference to her.

"You leave Clodhopper out of this," Christina half-grumbled, half-laughed. The woman had it all. A great fiancé, a fantastic house or...mansion might be a better word, and the ability to see the future whenever said ability decided to rear its not-always-friendly head. Hell, Aislinn had saved Kyle's life a few months back thanks to an early warning.

But once upon a time, she'd been in a very similar situation as Chris. Afraid of men because her sadistic ex-husband had stalked her with the intent to possess her no matter what it took. Chris didn't have an ex, she had a bastard of a father who drank too much and took out his anger with his fists. Usually on her mother's face. And yet, her mother loved the asshole and refused to leave him. Unlike Chris, who'd gotten out the first chance she'd had.

Aislinn sighed and set her tea down to take Chris's hand, uncurling her fingers from their fisted position to trap them between her own two hands. Her touch soothed Chris's tattered nerves, bringing her back from the direction her thoughts were taking her.

"I am so jealous of you, Ais."

Aislinn snorted. "Of what?"

"The way you got over your ex and embraced Kyle."

"Yes, well, my ex only thought he could control me. He didn't get drunk and beat me to a pulp and he certainly never groveled on his knees the next day, crying and apologizing for hitting me. Besides, Kyle is a pigheaded man who uses little things like mind-blowing orgasms to redirect me when I start thinking about the past."

"Must be nice."

"It is. You'll find it yourself one day, Chris."

Chris shrugged the consoling thought off, but found her gaze lifting to search the room. Two sets of piercing eyes connected with hers. She knew one was the blue of a cloudless sky and the other was so dark brown they were almost black. Both men straightened from the spots where they lounged near the bar and Chris swallowed. Two lean, muscle-packed bodies that could most likely break her in half easily. Why did she feel they would never do that to her? Maybe she felt their sense of honor from being in the military. Or maybe she'd seen them in action around other women, heard the rumors about how good they were in... No, she wasn't even going to go there.

A tingle of something wrapped around her. No way would she say it was awareness. She didn't want a man. Ever. Especially not one of those two.

"Much better." Aislinn patted her hand like she was a child.

"What's better?" Chris couldn't make herself look away. The men lifted their glasses in a mock salute, equally devilish grins gracing their faces. Her stomach somersaulted as she eyed their beverages held high. Beer? Something harder? It was too dim to tell across the distance.

"Your fingernails are no longer digging into my hand."

Chris gasped and, finally breaking the link between herself and TJ Mcfee and Jonathan Winslow, stared in horror at the damage she'd done to her best friend's skin.

"See?" Aislinn's lips curled at the corners. "Even if you don't want to admit it, your subconscious knows those guys won't hurt you."

Oh, good God, could Aislinn read minds too? "How in the hell do you figure that, Ms. Freud?" she huffed.

"Because from the minute you spotted them, your whole body relaxed."

Had it? Shit, Aislinn was right. Chris realized the tension was gone from her jaw and her Coke was no longer in danger of being smashed to smithereens. She jerked her gaze back to TJ and Jon. TJ had his thumbs hooked in the waistband of his jeans and Jon leaned negligently against the bar, his arms crossed over his chest.

Her heart thudded, this time for a reason other than fear of the half-tanked bodies surrounding her. Why? How could Aislinn see something Chris couldn't—or subconsciously wouldn't? Was it possible Chris actually felt something other than total disgust for the male species with TJ or Jon? If so, what, and for which one?

She sucked in a quick breath and changed the subject. "Where is Mr. Turner, anyway?"

"If Kyle heard you call him Mr. Turner he'd probably dock your pay somehow."

Chris laughed. "Sorry, but the man is my boss."

"Yes, but he's my fiancé and it's weird to hear you call him

Mr. Turner."

"You were calling him the same thing a few months ago."

"Touché."

"So, you didn't answer my question. Where is your man? I thought he and TJ and Jon were attached at the hips. Does your bed get crowded at night?" There was always attitude to hide behind when all else failed.

"Nope. Not at night, but sometimes it does on the mornings they run together. I swear when those guys come in all bare-chested and sweaty from their five-mile run, it's like slurping heaven. I just want to lick the three of them up."

"Shut up," Chris snarled. This time when her fingers tightened on the glass it had nothing to do with fear and everything to do with the green-eyed monster called jealousy, which was stupid since she knew Aislinn was teasing her. Kyle wouldn't let another man within a foot of Aislinn.

Chris's heart skipped a beat. She wasn't jealous. Couldn't be. Not over her best friend's obvious attempt at getting a rise out of her, and not about a man. Men. No.

Aislinn blinked and her lips curved up in a smile she tried to hide. "I thought you wanted to know. You asked."

"I didn't mean that and you know it." Chris snorted. "You've never licked the sweat off anyone but Kyle and I *don't* want to know about it."

"Ah, but you did want to know about TJ and Jon. Don't deny it, Chris. I may be the last person to be giving advice on men here, sweetie, but what can it hurt to give them a try? Have a fling, get them out of your system—if that's what needs to happen—and move on. Besides, you put on a skirt for them and let your hair down, you know you did."

Chris choked on her Coke. She had not put this skirt on for

them. She'd worn it because...well, it had been a moment of insanity that had urged her to take it out of her closet this morning and bring it to work to change into for this party. She had not been thinking about the way it flowed around her legs so nicely just above the knee. So nicely someone else might notice too. She hadn't. The hair thing wasn't for them either. She'd chosen to leave her long blonde strands down to float around her shoulders where it emphasized her slender neck and framed her heart-shaped face because the ponytail had been giving her a headache. Yeah. That was it.

Aislinn chuckled. "I can see the denial written all over your face and I must say, you're so full of shit your eyes are brown."

Chris snorted. "My eyes are always brown." Then Aislinn's words sank in. "Them? Them? What do you mean them? Jeez, can't I at least do one at a time?" Which one would that be? If anything was going to happen she'd have to choose one over the other, but how? Both had endearing qualities, both were God's gift to sex on a stick and... What the hell was she thinking? She didn't want either of them. She'd heard the rumors about them sharing a woman, yeah. Straight from Aislinn's mouth, even. Didn't make her believe them. Didn't make her want it so bad she could taste it. Why would any woman in the world want to put up with two men, for cripes sake?

Stop. Stop thinking. You don't want either one. You don't.

Aislinn's face wrinkled up. "I believe they come as a package deal."

"No way." How childish did that sound? From the corner of her eye she saw Jon straighten from his sprawl near the bar and step toward them. TJ moved with him. "Crap. They heard me didn't they? Did I really say it that loud?"

"Yes," Aislinn answered dryly.

Chris spun around, turning her back on them. "They're

coming."

Aislinn stood on tiptoe and peered over Chris's shoulder. "Uh-huh."

"Great. Shit. Shit, shit, shit. Why? Why are they coming?" She grasped Aislinn's arm with her free hand. She felt like a damn schoolgirl with a crush on her teacher she didn't want anyone to know about.

"I don't know, but stop spazzing out. Take a breath. In. Out. It might be because you said it loud enough to bring the roof down. Maybe they're worried about you?"

"Are you serious about them..." Chris gulped, "...sharing?" she hissed.

"Yes."

Chris's knees nearly buckled and enough heat pooled between her legs she had to fight the urge to rub her clit. What the *hell* was happening to her and why was it culminating now of all times?

"Hello ladies." Jon's gravelly voice sounded behind her a second before a hand landed on the small of her back.

Aislinn smiled at her, a big toothy grin that said she was pleased with what was happening. Chris straightened like an arrow and narrowed her eyes at her best friend. Had she planned this? She tried to think if that scenario was possible but came up empty. Aislinn hadn't given a two-fingered whistle and beckoned the men over. Chris hadn't even seen her make eye contact with them. Had to be all her own doing. She brought them to her with her idiotic loud voice.

This was not happening. Those warm fingertips were not burning a hole straight through her and making her want the touch on more pertinent parts of her anatomy. Her pulse was not racing a mile a minute and her nipples were not hardening into pencil-sharp points. And most of all, their smell was *not* enticing her to do things like turn around and sniff their necks.

"Hello, TJ, Jon," Aislinn said amiably. "Chris and I were just talking about Kyle."

"Ah. So that's what all the screaming was about." TJ moved to Chris's side with a chuckle.

He was laughing at her. "All the screaming? Two words. I inadvertently, and with a small amount of noise, said two words. All right, yelled. I yelled them. You act like I made a commotion."

"Oh, look, a table opened up. Let's sit, shall we?" Aislinn said, guiding them off topic and saving Chris from humiliating herself further. Aislinn took Chris's elbow and steered her to a round high table with three stools positioned around it. "How many chairs do we need, Jon?" She herded another seat from a nearby table.

Chris watched as Jon's glance took in the nice-sized room packed with almost all of Turner Industries' employees. What he was looking for, she didn't know. He and TJ had taken up residence, flanking her sides. Did they think she was going to make a break for it?

Probably. She thought she might too. Now looked good.

Jon put his hand on her back again and both he and TJ reached for the same chair and pulled it out. "I think just seven. Joe's here and Kyle and Marsha are on their way."

Chris found herself shepherded onto the high stool with the aid of one of their hands on each of her arms. Kind of made slipping away hard to do.

"Hey, there's Kyle now." Aislinn sounded so happy. A twinge of jealousy reared its ugly head again inside Chris's brain. She wanted to feel that way about a man someday too. She cocked her head. Maybe she should try lesbianism.

Nah. She didn't begrudge anyone their preference in lifestyles, she just didn't think it was right for her. Somehow she had to get over her fears and move on. Trust. It was all about trust.

Then again, maybe she already trusted someone. She peeked from the corner of her eye at TJ and then at Jon. Could it be? Did her body trust them even if her mind didn't? Is that why she didn't go all screwball with them near like she did with other men? She hadn't seen them display any kind of negative vibes at work, but then her dad had a public face too. One he wore in the light of day. Midday, after his hangover allowed him to creep out of bed.

Chris hated her father for giving her every reason in the world not to like men. Her brother, Carter, who was turning into the same kind of man as their father, and the two men she'd tried to have relationships with in the past had solidified her view of the species. Men were scum, plain and simple.

Aislinn, therefore, must have found the one and only penis that wasn't.

Either TJ's or Jon's cologne wafted under her nose. She pictured a cartoon-style trail of smoke creeping toward her. One end was curled into a hook, beckoning her like someone crooking their finger. It flooded her nostrils, forcing her to turn her head and look to the man it had come from. Jonathan. Those sky blue eyes glittered back at her and she had to swallow.

Okay, if she were truly honest with herself, maybe he made her want to try the whole relationship game again. With him, no one else. Maybe Aislinn was right. What could a fling hurt? Might get the burgeoning flame that flickered through her body whenever she looked at him out of her system.

She turned and faced TJ and felt the same flare of heat.

Crap.

Chris crossed her legs. It was damn hot in the bar if the sweat at her apex was anything to go by. Good thing she didn't wear pantyhose. She could practically feel the itchiness superimposed over her thighs, the tickling of nylon along her crotch.

She sprang upright. When, at any time in her life, had pantyhose ever made her crotch tingle? But if she had worn them, she could have blamed what she felt on them. What was wrong with her?

"Can we get you another drink? Teej is going up." Jon's words rumbled next to her ear, sending a shockwave of longing sweeping through her.

Her tummy flipped over. "Uh-uh." Was she answering him about the drink, or denying out loud that one, or possibly two, particular men were making her pussy tickle? Lord, maybe she wasn't even really sweating. Maybe she was...*creaming*?

Mortified at her own thoughts, she stared straight ahead and refused to look at Jon as she shook her head. Her pulse throbbed at the junction of her thighs. Right about the spot her clit would be—oh Lord, she had it bad. She wanted a man. Men, she conceded. She wanted both these men. Which only confirmed she wasn't as dead toward the male species as she would like to believe. It absolutely did not make her want to sacrifice herself to them. Wanting was one thing, doing another.

Joe Archer from Turner's design team ambled over. Joe was a prime example why she wouldn't act on her desires for anyone. From the look of the man, he had already overindulged. Chris sighed. Deep down inside she knew she wasn't being fair to the opposite sex. They weren't *all* like her father or Joe. Surely not every man on the face of the earth drank too much. She knew they didn't and it was unrealistic to think she'd never find one of them. It was also damn hard to get over the fears she'd experienced first-hand. The ones she'd lived with for most of her life.

She felt Jon press against her. Only the wooden chair back separated them and his hands landed on her shoulders in silent support.

How did he know?

He swiped aside the escaped tendrils of hair at her nape with his thumbs and dug in to knead the tense muscles at the base of her neck. Chris's spine melted, pushing her into his caress. He could give her a massage anytime.

You are losing your ever-loving mind. Hadn't she just convinced herself she would do nothing?

"He won't touch you, I promise." Jon's warm breath fanned over her cheek when he bent so only she could hear. She gave a slight nod, accepting for the moment that he spoke the truth. See? There it was, her body trusted him instinctively, a split second before she even realized what he'd said. What made her trust him she didn't know, but it felt right. Better than Joe's presence anyhow.

"Hey, sorry I'm late." Kyle pulled a stool out and helped Aislinn onto its high seat. Too bad there was a seat separating them because Chris really needed a female close by right now. Jonathan was quickly becoming too easy to be next to.

She tilted her head, semi-guiding Jon's fingers to a particular spot, and heard him chuckle.

"Marsha had to run home to a sick kid so she won't be here."

Rats. There went another XX chromosome. There was a conspiracy at work here tonight.

TJ returned just as Kyle hopped on his stool. TJ's hands

were full, carrying four glasses of various sizes containing pale to dark brews. He plunked them on the table and divvied them up between himself, Jon, Kyle and Aislinn.

"Thanks, Teej." Kyle took a sip and licked the foam from his upper lip before leaning over to kiss his fiancée. A second of intense longing flitted through Chris. Aislinn looked so happy with Kyle, smiling and wiping his beer kiss away. On second thought, there was no longing. Gas, maybe, like the smiles you find on infants, but not longing. Who would long to be beer kissed?

Joe threw his head back, capturing Chris's attention, and downed what was left in his glass. He'd been left out of TJ's drink run. Not that he needed another one. After devouring the remnants of one glass, he reached for a second one he'd brought with him.

Chris tensed again and Jon's fingers dug in, keeping her from rising off her stool like she wanted to. She half-expected him to say, "Stay."

Kyle raised his glass in salute. "Cheers."

Everyone lifted a glass above their head. Surely no one would notice how hers wobbled in the dim light.

"And here's to all the other Fortune 500 companies who switch their security needs to Turner Industries." Joe's slightly slurred voice boomed across the round wooden table. How long had he been drinking? And how long would it be before he turned inevitably violent?

They gave a chorus of "Here, heres" which Chris felt disinclined to participate in. She shivered and fought back the panic bubbling its way to the surface. Jon's fingers squeezed again, reassuring and adding comfort from a source she never thought she'd look toward. The man was wreaking havoc on her brain. From the seat he'd taken next to her, TJ covered the hand she had resting on her thigh with his own.

A small gesture no one would see but the three of them. *Everyone can see Jon standing behind you rubbing your shoulders, though.*

Kyle and Aislinn shared another kiss, this one deeper than their previous meeting of lips. Chris watched, mesmerized, as their tongues dueled. Joe cleared his throat, breaking the spell, but Chris continued to wonder, not for the first time, how Aislinn did it. From past to present, how had she swept her fears aside and moved on?

More importantly, how did Chris start letting men get close, knowing in the back of her mind there was always the potential for things to turn ugly? Chris's own mother was now a shell of a woman, unable to stand on her own. No, more like unwilling to. Chris had vowed long ago never to let a man treat her the way her father treated her mother.

Mouth suddenly dry thanks to memories, Chris took a gulp of her warm, still mostly full Coke. Her hand shook so bad, the dark liquid sloshed over the rim to trickle across her skin.

"Damn it." She winced and searched for a napkin. Seeing none, she set the glass down and licked the sticky soda. A low growl made her jump.

"Need some help?" TJ's head came perilously close to her hand, his mouth open, tongue hanging out.

Chris pushed him away with two fingers on his forehead. "No, stud, I do not need your help." Mortified at having called TJ a stud, Chris slapped her palm over her mouth. Her cheeks flared with heat. She normally hid behind a "fuck off" attitude, which these two always seemed to bring out, but under the current damp-panty issue, now was not the time to be calling either one a stud. Both of them would misinterpret her meaning.

"Stud? I'm moving up in the world." TJ snaked an arm between her back and Jon's front to lie along her chair back. His fingertips grazed her upper arm, leaving goose bumps.

"Wrong, bud." She scooted forward, hunching over the table. No man would move up in her world.

Why was that thought starting to sound delusional? Resisting the urge to fan herself and possibly give TJ more ammunition, she took a long drink of Coke to try to dissipate the heat steadily building up inside her.

"What's wrong?" Jon curled his upper body over her, doubling her heart rate.

Chris looked over her shoulder to see TJ wiggling his eyebrows.

"She called me a stud."

Double damn. She slumped forward. Maybe she could knock herself out and chalk this whole situation up to a dream. Her head hit the table with a thud. "Owwwwchie."

She heard a smack above her head. They were giving high fives? Great. "Go away," she grumbled, sitting back up.

"Never," Jon whispered.

He really needed to stop doing that. It made her whole body prickle with need. Her heart pounded, with fear or excitement she wasn't sure, but suspected the latter. The weird little tickle sliding from her tummy down to her clit only served to confirm her suspicions. This feeling was one of the reasons she lay awake nights.

The ones she spent lying in bed, envisioning TJ or Jon caressing her skin with their mouths, licking and nibbling their way to her mound. More often than not, she wound up inserting her fingers into her tight, sopping passage wondering what it would feel like to have one of their cocks filling her. Just once she wanted to give up and let a man take control of her body and give her what she'd only read about in fiction. Maybe with them... Could she? Should she? The prospect was looking more and more appealing. She could drive her own car, get away if she needed to. It would for damn sure be easier driving off than kicking them out of her house. And surely they wouldn't hurt someone they worked with, would they? Aislinn had said, "Have a fling, get it out of your system." Chris could do this. She would. Tonight. If they wanted to, that was.

This time she did fan herself by waving her hand. A pitiful amount of air wafted across her face. "It's hot in here, isn't it?"

"Have a drink." There was a definite smile in Jon's voice. He stepped to her side, opposite the side TJ occupied, and grabbed his own drink. Before she knew what was happening, he tilted the glass to her lips. It was drink or drown.

Shock nearly choked her. Two hands thumped her back between her shoulder blades as she spluttered.

"Soda." She cringed at how stupid she must sound.

"What else would it be, baby?" Jon twirled a lock of her hair around his finger.

Chris stared at him. Had he lost his mind? They were at a party on a Friday night, happy hour no less. Did she look like a complete moron? How many people besides her were drinking anything other than alcohol? A few, maybe. There was a pregnant woman from Human Resources at a nearby table.

TJ's lips brushed her ear. If those puppies got any more attention tonight she was afraid they might fall off. They'd been whispered against, breathed on, sniffed and now kissed.

"Alcohol upsets you, so why would we drink it?" TJ asked as if it were already clear they wouldn't drink around her.

Chris's stomach took a dive and her throat closed.

"Breathe, sugar."

She did, sucking in a deep breath only to hold it again. Two soothing palms rubbed her back. "How did you know?" she rasped. They couldn't know. Unless Aislinn had told them. Chris turned to her friend. Her face held a glimpse of sympathy Chris didn't find comforting, but the mouthed words, "I didn't do it," helped.

"Aislinn didn't tell us anything, Chris. Don't blame her. Hey." Jon tilted her face toward his with his thumb under her chin. "Does it matter *how* we know? What really matters is that we do and that you know we'll never drink around you."

Her whole body shaking, she laughed at him. She couldn't help it. The peal came from somewhere deep inside, bringing tears to her eyes. Jon's hand slipped from her chin to the back of her neck. He pulled her close and hugged her tight.

"Did I say something funny?" His chest rumbled against her cheek.

For a split second she felt safe. More so, she felt cherished and protected, like nothing would ever happen to her in the shelter of his arms.

Then she recovered and pushed away. TJ had scooted closer so there wasn't far to go. Chris straightened her spine and lifted her chin. "My father never drank around us either."

Chapter Two

"Your father is a fucking moron." Jon sighed when Chris gasped and tried to jerk farther away. He had wanted to get her fears out in the open, just not in this particular environment. A room full of witnesses had not been his ideal, but establishing that he and TJ would never drink around her was first and foremost in earning her trust. He also knew she wouldn't have come if they'd had this party at a bar like Kyle had originally wanted. Jon and Teej had vetoed his plans immediately.

The last thing they wanted was for her to stay away from a company party based on its location. Especially when the minx was proving to be a bit stubborn in the subtle flirtation department. It was time to bring out the big guns, but short of kidnapping her and thus terrifying her, they had to woo. Wooing wasn't as easy as it looked. Not when it involved someone with a past like Chris's. Jon would give anything to wipe the look of unease from her face right now. A wild romp in bed might cure it.

Everything else revolved around her trust in them. Without it, they had nothing, and nothing was out of the question. He and TJ were determined to make Chris theirs in every way possible. If she started out thinking they only wanted a fling, they would quickly disillusion her.

Jon wished they were anywhere but here. They needed somewhere they could talk in private. But he'd known from the get-go she wouldn't just up and leave with them. It would take time and planning and a little help from her best friend Aislinn. Since he knew getting Chris here was half the battle, he'd implored Aislinn to help. Whatever she'd done or said to Chris had worked. Seeing her walk in with that flowing skirt just about knocked the breath from his lungs. His dick was rock hard and this close to her, smelling her, it was near to exploding without even being touched.

He knew there'd be a battle easing her into their lifestyle. Hell, half the battle would be seeing to her comfort around men in general. She had nice diversionary tactics, hiding behind her attitude or flirting from a distance. None of which fazed him or TJ in the least. There wasn't much in the world that could faze two ex Special Forces team members and they for damn sure weren't going to back down without a fight.

Jon swiped his thumb across one of her pink cheeks, counting it as a victory when she didn't flinch or pull away. He couldn't wait to see them flushed with the pleasure he and TJ would grace upon her. Would she scream out one or both of their names? Was she the silent type, a moaner? Based on the rapid pulse at her throat, he could tell she wasn't as unaffected by him as she would like to think she was.

"The difference between your father and TJ and I is that we won't drink, *ever.*" He enunciated very clearly, giving her no room to misinterpret. "If there's ever a time you don't feel comfortable, you just have to tell us."

She snorted. "I'm not comfortable. Back off." She raised her hands and pushed at his chest in an attempt to create space between them. He gave her a modicum and laughed. They'd never get anywhere if they let her have her way every time.

The shrill ring of a cell phone interrupted them. Chris never took her gaze off him. The phone rang again and she lifted her glass and sipped. TJ moved closer. "You gonna answer that?"

Chris did a double take. "What?"

"Your pocket is ringing, sugar," Jon offered.

"Huh? Oh. Oh, crap." She fumbled in the pocket of her skirt for the slim pink flip phone he knew she carried.

He just smiled. She was fucking gorgeous when riled, which was most of the time around them. They seemed to bring it out of her in spades. There was the flush, this time from frustration. Soon it would be courtesy of an explosive orgasm given by him or Teej.

"Hello?" She stuck a finger in her ear to drown out the noise. "Carter? Is that you?"

Carter. Chris's younger brother, who, from Jon's background search into the Marshall family, seemed to follow in Daddy's footsteps. At least in the mean department. Christina had done the smart thing, getting away from her family.

"No, I do not have any money."

TJ stood, exchanging a knowing look over her head with Jon. They both disliked the tone they heard in her voice.

"Well, geez, I don't know, Carter. Get a job like everyone else in the world maybe?" She paused and her eyes widened. "I will never fund your disgusting habit. I work too hard for the money I earn to waste it on you."

Shit. If the kid had a habit and needed money for a fix, things could get ugly fast. Faster if he owed money he didn't have.

A second later her eyes narrowed into slits. "You leave Mother out of this." She paused. "I already regret it." She slammed the flip closed and growled.

"Carter's bothering you again?" Aislinn asked across the table.

"Again?" TJ and Jon barked together. Jon saw red. If the little punk had taken to messing with Chris, Jon would put an end to it really quickly.

"He says he needs money to pay his rent."

"And you know he's lying, right?" Aislinn came around the table, nudging Jon out of the way with a sharp elbow to his stomach. He stepped back with an oomph while TJ and Kyle snickered. He flipped them both off.

"After last month? Yes, I know."

"What the hell happened last month?" TJ snarled. Jon wanted to know the exact same thing and more. Like how they'd missed her brother's problems when running a background check on her, something they did with everyone who worked for their company. Chris's had been a little more involved since both of them knew she would inevitably end up in their bed. With their past in the Teams, it was both a habit and a necessity. He, Teej and Kyle had pissed off more than one baddy out there who would stop at nothing to seek revenge. A loved one would be an easy target.

Before Chris could answer, Aislinn said, "Carter drove all the way from Chicago and showed up at her door begging for money for some overdue bill he had. When she offered to take him to the phone company to pay it for him, he flipped out saying he could handle it on his own. Then he tore through her house, grabbed her wallet and stole all the cash she had in there."

"Motherfucker." Jon wanted to put his fist through a wall. Or better yet, Carter's face. "Why the fuck didn't you tell us?"

Chris drew back, one eyebrow raised high. She crossed her arms over her chest. "Why would I?"

Damn. Why would she? They didn't exactly have a relationship. Yet.

Starting right now, they did and he'd be goddamned if he let her junkie of a brother run roughshod over her again.

"Oh, I don't know, maybe so we could help?"

"I think I can handle my own brother."

Jon snorted. "You handled him so well he ran you over to steal your money. How much did he get?"

"I don't see how it's any of your—"

"How much?"

"A hundred and twenty bucks."

Feeling the muscle ticking along his jaw, he nodded once. "Do you think you've heard the last of him tonight?"

"I don't know. What does it matter?"

"You matter," Jon growled and leaned closer so she had no choice but to look him in the eye. "TJ and I are done waiting for you." He saw the flash of heat flare in her eyes. Hell, he could smell the moisture pooling between her legs. She could deny it all she wanted, but her body craved what he and Teej could offer. "We're not like your father or your brother and the only way you'll see that is to let us close. Probably won't be easy for you, but I can damn well guarantee it'll be worth it."

Her eyes widened, her nostrils flared with each inhalation, and the pulse at the base of her throat sped up. He wanted to lean in and lick it, to taste her and leave his mark. Not here though. He straightened. If his dick got any harder, he'd be popping out of his jeans. Wouldn't that be something?

"I don't"—she had to clear her throat—"I don't know what you're talking about."

"Sex, Chris. Remember the conversation we were having earlier?" Aislinn butt in.

"*Aislinn.*" Chris's hissed reprimand made Jon laugh out loud. Oh God the woman was priceless. He'd wondered what they'd been talking about when she'd yelled out across the bar.

"What?" Aislinn said innocently. "I'm just getting you back for a little incident that happened at work a couple of months ago. Remember there was something about a feather duster?"

"That was your fault. You're the one who asked Kyle if he had a duster but didn't expound on what kind, or that we'd been imagining them wearing dusters, cowboy hats and nothing el— Oh my God." Chris's eyes closed. "Please tell me I didn't just say that out loud."

"What kind of conversation were you having, Ais?" TJ grinned like a loon.

"I told her to have an affair, get it over with."

Jon was sure by the murderous look on Chris's face Aislinn was in line for a not-so-quick, painful death. Time to get Chris out of here.

TJ snorted. "I'm not looking for an affair."

"Me neither," Jon grunted.

Chris swung her startled gaze back and forth between them. Aislinn smiled sweetly.

Somewhere Chris found her voice, but what came out wasn't what Jon expected. A wounded, embarrassed look overtook her features. "Well. I wasn't looking for an affair either." She hopped off the stool and took off toward the door.

"Ah hell," TJ muttered.

Jon cut off her flight. "Never said nothing about not wanting you, Christina, just said I wasn't looking for an *affair*." Her back went ramrod straight as she halted in mid-stride.

She looked back over her shoulder and Jon saw the sheen of tears in her eyes. Fuck.

"Teej, it's time to go."

"Yep." TJ slapped some bills on the table and saluted Kyle.

Jon never took his gaze off Chris. She swallowed and he'd bet his Beamer sitting outside her nipples were hard as rocks.

"See you Monday, Kyle," he said, insinuating with his tone they didn't want to be disturbed for the rest of the weekend. It was past time for them to start showing her they could be trusted with her life. He couldn't wait.

TJ met Chris where she'd come to a dead stop and took hold of her elbow.

"What are you doing?" Her not-so-outraged squeak didn't even turn heads.

"Escorting you to the car, ma'am." TJ grinned again. The man could melt butter with that grin. Jon had long ago decided it was one of the reasons women were so attracted to him.

"But I came with Ais—"

"Guys. Hold up," Aislinn called and hurried over to them. "'Scuse us a sec, huh?" She grabbed Chris's hand and retreated, pulling Chris with her.

"Chris, I want you to know I will back you one hundred percent if you don't want this, it's just, I can see how you look at them at work and I *know* from overhearing them with Kyle they want you, and if you hate me forever for having sprung this on you, that's okay, but"—Jon could see Aislinn wince and hear every word she said—"I kinda, sorta gave 'em the keys to your house because they said they wanted a few things to make you more comfortable with them and damn, this whole thing is all my fault and I'm sorry."

So far Chris hadn't been able to get a word in edgewise. Jon put his weight on one leg and waited, holding his breath for her response. If she said no, they'd turn around and leave and never bring it up again. Until next time, anyway. He couldn't see her face but her shoulders slumped and Jon knew they'd been defeated. TJ must have felt the same.

"Come on, man, let's go." TJ's voice was detached and flat.

"Can you take a breath now? Sheesh," Chris muttered. Jon stood straighter, hope sparking to life. TJ's hand fisted in the shirt at Jon's shoulder. He'd heard too.

"The truth is... God I can't believe I'm saying this, but I think I want this too. How will I ever know if I can make something work if I don't try and maybe these two are safe, ya know? Because of work and all?"

Safe? Jon wanted to howl at the moon. Fuck yeah they were safe. He'd give her his gun if he had to, to prove how safe they were.

"Are you hearing what I'm hearing?" TJ growled in his ear.

"Yep."

"Will you come get me if it doesn't...you know, if I freak out or something? Maybe you could hang out in your car. Oh, God, what am I doing, Ais?" Chris groaned.

Aislinn grinned from ear to ear. "You're doing what feels right, Chris, believe in that. I know you, you wouldn't get near this situation with a hundred-foot pole if it didn't make you feel right inside."

Chris shrugged. It took everything Jon had not to go to her, to give her the time she needed to come to them. If she turned around right now and said she only wanted to talk, they'd take it. They would hate it and have to relieve major cases of blue balls another way, but they'd take it. Anything to get her to feel comfortable with them.

"You're right." Chris nodded sharply once and Jon saw her shoulders rise with the deep breath she took. "I can do this. I *want* to do this. I'm going to have sex."

Jon smiled and wondered if she knew they could hear her. She twisted and looked back over her shoulder and her face colored a pretty dark shade of pink indicating that she probably knew now. She faced Aislinn again and he heard her mutter, "They heard me say I wanted to have sex, didn't they?"

"I think so, sweetie." Aislinn tried not to smile. Jon had to give her credit. She failed miserably but she tried.

"Fine. I guess I'm stuck then. I'm going to have sex." She peeked behind her again and Jon saw her swallow as her gaze tracked from him to TJ. His cock couldn't get any harder. "Apparently twice," she murmured.

Oh, baby, I guarantee it'll be more than twice, Jon thought.

"Go with them. You know I'll come get you if I need to but Kyle trusts them with his life and I have a feeling you can too. They're honorable men, Chris."

Chris sighed and faced them head on. Jon held a hand out, palm up, his heart thudding in anticipation. Tonight they'd show her not only how fantastic the three of them would be together in bed, but that she could trust them with her body and spirit as well.

Chris straightened her spine and lifted her chin. Jon had to laugh. She looked like she'd resigned herself to walking the plank. He and TJ were about to show her the heights they could take her to when she stepped off. She moved, marching toward his outstretched hand with complete determination and a glitter of heat in her eyes. Her nostrils flared as she reached out and put her hand—and even if she didn't realize it, her trust—in the palm of his hand.

"Where are we going?" she whispered.

"Home." Jon tugged her out the door with TJ on her other side and led them to his car, glad she had come with Aislinn and they didn't have to worry about hers. Leaning back, he eyeballed her shapely legs beneath her skirt, something he'd never seen her in. Sexy as all get out. His gaze wandered higher to her firm butt and lack of...

"Are you not wearing any panties, Chris?" Risky for a woman afraid of men; damn lucky for him and TJ. Yet thinking about what could have happened with just about any man at the party tonight made his head spin. He didn't mind her not wearing panties in their presence, hell, he'd welcome it with open arms, but around other dicks, no way.

"I don't think that's any of your business," she huffed, staring straight ahead and refusing to look at him. In the darkening twilight of late evening, Jon could see her cheeks infuse with color.

"It'll be my business soon, sugar."

"You think so?"

Jon stopped her next to his car, turning her slowly in his arms and backing her against the rear panel. He leaned in close and nibbled at her ear. "I know so."

TJ stood nearly as close, both of them crowding her yet giving her enough space to escape if she needed to. "Are we talking lack of panties here? 'Cause if we are, I'd like to put my two cents in."

Chris shoved at him, a tiny smile turning the corners of her mouth. "There is no lack of panties," she hissed and started to reach for the hem of her skirt.

TJ put his hand on hers to stop her and moved to her neck with his lips to nibble along her throat. "Don't worry, I'll take care of that little problem." She shivered and tilted her head, silently and willingly giving him better access. Her hands lifted to their chests and fisted, one on each of their shirts instead of pushing them away.

TJ zoned in on her mouth. Jonathan watched his best friend and the woman they both loved kiss and couldn't wait to take TJ's place. Her lips parted and meshed with TJ's. Jon shifted his stance, allowing his erection a millimeter of space against his zipper and withdrew a black strip of silk from his pocket. Chris angled her head to allow TJ better access. It was Jon's cue to step forward. He moved to her side and palmed the back of her head. She moaned as TJ's tongue slipped between her teeth.

"My turn," Jon growled. TJ backed off and Jon guided her mouth to his. He tasted both her and Teej. She whimpered into his mouth and he took hold of her hand and placed it on his cock, feeding off the small victory of her not pulling away.

Jon dropped his head to her forehead. "See what you fucking do to me, Christina? I want inside this sweet little pussy." He punctuated his words by easing his hand up her thigh beneath the skirt to her mound. His fingers skated over her soaking panties, pushing the fabric into her slit. Chris bit down on her lip.

"That's it, baby. Feel his hands on you?" TJ pinched a nipple between hers and Jon's bodies.

"Unh." Her fingers grasped him through denim and his cock threatened to explode right then and there.

They had to get the fuck home. He didn't want to take her in the parking lot.

Jon grasped her cheeks in his hands, the silk blindfold still in his grip, and turned her face up to his. He placed a kiss on her nose and gave himself a second to cool off before he said, "Give us the weekend, sugar. I guarantee you'll never want to leave."

Chris swallowed and her gaze darted between him and TJ.

"Okay." She closed her eyes.

God what he wouldn't give to lay her in the backseat, spread her thighs and thrust into her heat.

"Okay?" He bent his knees so he could stare right into her face and waited until she nodded. "Then choose a safe word."

"Huh?"

"A safe word, baby," TJ interjected. "Something you can say when you want us to back off. The second you say it, we stop whatever it is we're doing."

One of her eyebrows shot upward. "What exactly do you think it is we're gonna do that I'm gonna need a safe word for?"

"Whatever. Doesn't matter. You don't want to hold my hand, say the safe word." TJ nuzzled her cheek. "Don't like the way my tongue feels on your clit? Say the safe word."

Chris's entire body shivered in response and Jon could see her nipples harden beneath her blouse. "Take off the panties, Chris." There was only so much of this he could take.

Her eyes flew wide open. "Wha—what about my word?"

"Pick one," he growled.

"Asparagus," she shot back.

For a second Jon was dumbfounded. Only Chris would pick an astonishingly disgusting vegetable for a safe word.

"Fine. Asparagus. I'm not gonna ask again. Take off the panties and hand them to Teej." He winked at her. "I promise, he'll keep 'em safe."

A hundred emotions filtered across her face, but in the end, her own desire won out. He took a half step back, shielding her from anyone who might walk by as she lifted her skirt and peeled her panties down her legs.

"Good girl."

She blinked and handed the wadded pair of cotton to TJ, her cheeks fire engine red. TJ brought them to his face and inhaled deeply. Hell, even Jon could smell her essence and he didn't have them pressed to his nose. She was more than ready to take the two of them inside her.

"Spread your legs." Jon nestled his nose in the skin right below her ear. After a moment's hesitation she did as he asked and turned her feet in and out, separating them until they were about a foot apart. This time when he smoothed his hand up her leg, he met naked, soaked flesh.

"You're wet, Chris," he murmured.

TJ's hand joined his and she gasped. They each grabbed a thigh and coaxed her legs wider, then returned to her pussy. Jon stroked over her puffy lips.

"What color are you here, sugar? Dark pink? More mauve?" He dipped his tongue into her ear and felt TJ penetrate her sheath with a finger.

"Oh Jesus." Her body lifted onto her toes and her head fell back, exposing the column of her throat. Jon attacked, locking his lips onto the delicate skin and sucking it strongly into his mouth, leaving a mark for everyone to see and claiming her at the same time.

"Feel good?" TJ used his other hand to brush the hair off her face.

Jon sought out the bundle of nerves at the top of her slit and pulled back the hood covering it. He captured her cry with his mouth and rubbed tiny circles around the swollen nub. She was slippery wet with a copious amount of juice. TJ's finger thrust in and out, drawing more from her pussy.

It wouldn't be long. Chris's clit seemed to expand under his ministrations and her breath came in shallow pants. Her eyes, when she could open them, revealed dilated pupils and she fairly danced on her toes.

"Please." She shook her head, a myriad of emotions

crossing her face. “No. I can’t, umm, stop.” The muscles in her neck corded and she braced herself with a hand on each of their shoulders. “Oh my God. Shit. Asparagus,” she blurted.

Jon ripped his hand from between her soft thighs. TJ did the same. Both of them were breathing hard but nothing would make them do anything to compromise the semi-trust they were starting to build.

“Damn. Shit. Oh, God, I, uh. I just... I can’t do this.”

Jon hung his head and sucked in a deep breath.

“Here,” she yelped. “I mean, here. I can’t do this here, in the parking lot. It’s weird and”—she peered over their shoulders—“people can see us,” she panted.

TJ snorted. “I believe you’ve found the world’s quickest way to deflate an erection, baby.”

“Oh. Oh, I’m sorry. I don’t want you to stop...touching me. That was good, that was, well, fabulous, but I haven’t done this in awhile and...I’m not an exhibitionist,” she spat out.

“Ah, sugar.” Jon sighed. They’d gotten carried away and tried to take her in a goddamn parking lot like a couple of horny teenagers. How could he be such a fuckhead? With everything they knew about her past, here they were stripping her down in public, fingering her and getting ready to fuck her against the car.

Chris smiled. “Maybe we can get in the car at least?”

“Abso-fucking-lutely,” TJ agreed.

“Phew. I was worried you might change your minds.”

TJ yanked the back door open. “Never.” He tugged Chris around so her back was to his front, but before he helped her into the car Jon swept the blindfold over her eyes and tied it in the back.

“What are you doing?” The near panic in her voice gave Jon

second thoughts but TJ stepped in.

"Relax, baby." He clasped the hands she'd raised to the blindfold and brought them down. "I want your full attention while we're in the car. Trust me, this will make your senses soar." TJ lifted her knuckles and kissed them gently.

Her body softened and Jon's heart thudded against his ribs. Her submission meant the world to them. Not that they wanted her to cower to them, but to be relaxed enough to trust them never to hurt her.

"Whatever you do, please, please don't tie me down," she whispered. The heartfelt plea seemed to come from the bottom of her soul.

Jon would kill to have her tied to their bed, spread so they could take their turns with her. He glanced at TJ while he finished tying the knot. TJ shrugged in confusion.

Jon soothed her by running his palms down her sides until she shivered and leaned into him. He hugged her close and nestled his chin in the crease of her neck and shoulders.

"We will never hurt you, Christina."

She turned her face toward his. "It's not that," she admitted. "I..."

Jon lifted her chin and kissed her lips gently. "You what?"

She sighed. "I'm claustrophobic. I can't stand being in tight spaces or held so I can't move." She spoke so fast her words got strung together.

TJ barked out in laughter and Chris huffed. "It's not funny, TJ McFee." Even blindfolded she was able to recognize TJ from Jon.

Jon smiled.

"You're right, it's not, baby. No tying you up, I promise." TJ released her hands and put his on top of her head to help her into the backseat. “Not yet anyway,” he mumbled.

“I heard that,” she yelled.

Still chuckling, TJ followed her into the car. Jon slammed the door shut behind them and jogged around to the front. She would make things interesting, that was for sure. And hell, if they couldn’t tie her up—yet—there were a million other things they could do with and to her body.

Grinning in anticipation, Jon cranked the car and sped out of the parking lot.

Her pussy had to be leaving a wet spot on the leather beneath her butt. Chris licked her lips and dug her fingernails into her skirt. The blindfold tickled her nose. She lifted her chin and tried to peer underneath the edge. Nothing but pitch blackness surrounded her.

TJ laughed beside her and she blew out a breath. She should be panicking. Her heart should be racing. They were essentially kidnapping her, whether or not she’d gone along with it. They’d semi-promised not to tie her up—one of her biggest fears, along with elevators and trunks and the backseats of cars with only two doors. She had this insane phobia of going over a bridge in one of those deathtraps and not being able to get out. Sitting here, blindfolded, with two men who’d almost made her come with their fingers in a parking lot for all the world to see wasn’t making her bubble into hysteria. Well actually, it was—in anticipation of what was to come. She had a feeling what had started to happen against the car door was the tip of the iceberg.

Calloused fingers landed above her knee and she jumped.

“Easy, baby.” TJ smoothed his hand up her leg, lifting the skirt and easing his way to her core.

Chris spread her knees, allowing him access. Easy access.

Lord what the hell had happened to the woman who'd gone into work this morning intent on keeping the men of the universe at bay yet another day? She had turned into a lush of ginormous proportions.

His hand disappeared.

"Hey," she protested, then bit her lip. Did her giving in to him turn him off? Should she play hard to get? She'd been doing that for months now. She didn't want to do it anymore.

Their kisses must have sucked all her normal, rational reasoning from her head, leaving her a wanton.

TJ snorted. "I'm just repositioning you, Chris. Give me a sec."

Huh? Fabric rustled on the seats, sending a swirl of a leather scent puffing around her nose. She turned to the sounds he made while he moved. The air conditioner hummed. Goose bumps prickled along her bare arms and legs and her nipples hardened. She squirmed in the seat as they rubbed against her bra. What was he doing? What did he have planned? What the hell could he possibly think to do in the cramped backseat?

His hand cupped her beneath the knee closest to him and lifted, pulling and twisting her around until her back was pressed up against the door and her bent left leg rested on the upright of the seat. The position left her wide open. Heat flooded her face at what she knew he could see. One leg on the floor, the other raised and pushed back. Her skirt slid to her waist and the cool air enveloping them washed over her pussy lips. She groaned and lifted her hips, wanting something tangible to touch her. He was right. The blindfold increased her other senses tenfold.

TJ grabbed the hand farthest from him and balanced her forearm on the armrest of the door. The other arm he placed along the top of the headrest to her left.

"Don't move either one of them, Chris, or there will be consequences."

The car veered to the right and then back to the left as if Jon tried to avoid hitting something in the road.

"I'm fucking driving up here. Don't say things like that."

Her heart pounded with the implication but she couldn't help but smile at Jon's reaction. She was half tempted to move an arm just to find out what the consequences would entail. She licked her lips and gripped whatever she could reach without moving instead. Somehow, someway, she felt the heat of TJ's gaze on her exposed pussy. Her juices leaked from her, preparing her for whatever he'd chosen to do. When long seconds went by and nothing happened, she gave in and did the one thing she thought she'd never do with a man. She begged.

"TJ." Her voice cracked.

"Yes?"

Damn him. He knew what he was doing to her. She felt a flush creep over her chest and face and itched to move, to do anything in order to get him to stroke her with those fingers she could still feel deep inside her sheath. Her stomach ached with needing him.

"Touch me," she snapped, startling a bark of laughter from him. She almost ripped the blindfold off so she could look him in the eye when she slapped him.

Good Lord she'd gone from pushing men away to pleading in less than an hour. How did these two affect her the way they did?

"I'm admiring the view here, Chris."

She felt the air move as he leaned closer.

"These puffy lips of yours are shiny wet." He slipped a

finger down her drenched slit and she gasped and arched into him, nearly impaling herself on the single digit. TJ clucked his tongue and the finger went bye-bye, causing her to sob.

"No moving, remember?"

How could she flippin' forget? There would be permanent gouges in the expensive leather by the time they got to their home with the way she'd dug her fingers in. She couldn't quite contain her usual attitude.

"Actually, the 'them' you asked not to move referred to my arms, and I have not moved them."

A sharp slap landed on her pussy. Her reactive scream came out more like a squeak. She sucked in a breath, at first from the unexpected pain and then because of the way it made her squirm for him to do it again.

"We shoulda gagged her too, J."

"Sounds like it," Jon grunted from the front seat.

"Absolutely not," Chris stammered. She refused to be gagged. No way.

TJ's hand caressed up her shin, over her knee and down her thigh. Thank God she'd shaved this morning. It all came down to the godforsaken skirt now tousled around her waist. She probably wouldn't have shaved if she hadn't wanted to wear it tonight. Now she was so glad she had. His thumb came to rest on her clit.

"We've granted you your one request and promised not to tie you up. There was nothing said about not gagging you," he growled.

This time she did sob, crying out as the pad of his thumb rubbed too softly on the bundle of nerves. She needed more, harder, faster, deeper. Something! God, she was turning into a nympho.

"I'm going to taste you, Christina. I'm going to run my tongue along this pretty pink slit and lap up every bit of your cream." He emulated what his words said with a finger. "And when I'm good and ready, then I'll work on this little button." He circled her clit once more and the back of her head hit the window. "You are not to make a sound."

She whimpered and received a pinch to one of her lower lips. Chris pursed her mouth and breathed through her nose. If shutting the hell up would get him to go down on her, she'd shut the hell up.

A few seconds later she was rewarded. The tip of his tongue did exactly what he'd said it would, gliding along her pussy from anus to clit and back again. A tiny moan escaped her throat and TJ left her high and dry. She could have cried. Only the sounds of the tires on the road, the whirring of the air conditioner and their breathing filled the car. She still could have heard a pin drop.

"I'm sorry," she whispered. "I've never done anything like this before." They had to understand. She'd never *wanted* to do anything like this before. "Give me a chance. I'll get better, I swear."

A palm cupped her cheek and she angled her head into it.

"I don't doubt you for a minute, baby."

Chris let out the breath she didn't realize she'd been holding. His voice sounded so sincere.

"That's the last time I tell you, Chris."

Chris froze at TJ's words, waiting for the fear, the panic. It didn't come. Something else happened though. Something she'd never be able to explain. Her clit throbbed. She actually felt the traitorous little bundle of nerves throb in anticipation.

Your body knows what it wants and who to trust even if your mind doesn't.

Was it true? Had to be, because nothing about TJ's gruff announcement made her feel the least bit uncomfortable. All right it did, but not in the afraid-for-her-life kind of way. It made her want him and everything he could give. Everything *they* could give her, and she wanted it now. Badly.

The flat of TJ's tongue swiped through her pussy again and each agitated thought fled her mind. Her brain became mush with every pass of his mouth on her clit. He swirled and dipped inside her vagina then moved lower to circle her anus.

Her eyes rolled back behind the blindfold. Never had anyone touched her there and oh my God, if he didn't do it again… Yes. It was the most erotic thing. Not something she ever imagined doing and yet, it felt so damn good. Who knew? Her clit pulsed and grew. Her nipples hardened and rubbed against her bra. She wanted to be naked. She wanted TJ's cock inside her. Right now.

God. She couldn't believe she was doing this.

His tongue moved to lick at her clit and his fingers pulled back the hood. Despite his warning of retribution, she couldn't not move. Her hips jerked in time with his licks, pushing closer to his mouth. She was so close, so close, so—

Chris screamed. The orgasm tore through her body like an explosion. Her thighs shook and her fingers ground into the leather as she held on until the end. She panted and waited for her body's systems to slow down. She didn't even know the car had come to a stop.

The door behind her opened. She yelped and would have spilled out if whoever it was at her back hadn't caught her. She was lifted from the car and carried to wherever they'd stopped.

"You're lucky I didn't stop along the side of the road to fuck you, sugar." Jon held her. His chest rumbled gruffly along her side, stiffening her nipples into tighter points. The damn things were likely to pop if this continued. “As soon as I get you inside this door, prepare to have my cock buried in that pussy TJ just enjoyed.”

“Can I speak now?”

She heard a key jammed in a lock and a knob turned. The door thudded like it had been kicked and with swift strides she was shifted and turned. Her back hit a wall.

“No. You can fuck now.”

Chapter Three

Jon wrapped her legs around his waist, inhaling the remnants of her orgasm. Driving while TJ had gone down on her had been sheer torture. More than twice he'd almost driven off the road while trying to watch them in the rearview mirror.

Her cheeks were flushed, her lungs heaving, and the tip of her tongue poked out to wet her upper lip. Soon it would be the engorged head of his cock she touched with her tongue.

He rested his forehead on hers, pressed her into the wall with his body and reached between them to unzip. His cock was thick and hard and weeping with pre-come. He stripped her shirt over her head, careful not to dislodge the blindfold. "I've been waiting for this moment for months," he growled, and captured her gasp of shock with his mouth.

Jon devoured her. He pressed his knee between her legs to support her and cradled her face in his hands. Sweeter than honey. He bet a million bucks her pussy would be even sweeter.

His dick twitched between them, ready to be buried in her heat. "I can't wait for a bed, Christina." He caressed his thumbs over her cheeks, wanting her to feel that he would never hurt her. It had been a long time for her and he was a big man. Penetrating her tight little pussy might take some time.

Time he would enjoy immensely, more so if she did too. He reached into his back pocket and retrieved the condom he'd stashed there. He and TJ hadn't been positive they would make it home and above all else, they meant to protect her.

Not that he wouldn't love to see Chris round with either his or TJ's baby, but not yet. Not until they'd fully gained her trust.

Jon bunched the skirt she wore up around her waist and, tearing open the foil pack with his teeth, sheathed himself.

She caught her bottom lip with her teeth and he could tell she was thinking. What she finally whispered surprised him. "I don't want you to wait."

He had expected she might need some major time to adjust to them this weekend. What had changed? Her hands tentatively settled on his shoulders before smoothing down to his abdomen.

Jon bit back a groan. Her fingers feathered over his T-shirt-covered belly as if searching for something. He had a feeling he knew exactly what she was looking for but if she touched him it would all be over.

"Uh-uh." He grabbed her hands and placed them high on the wall, holding both her tiny wrists in one of his big hands. The action raised her breasts almost as if in invitation. One he readily accepted by flicking open the front closure of her bra and swooping in to suck one tight nipple into his mouth.

"Damn, you don't waste time, do you?" TJ chuckled as he walked in behind them.

Jon let go with a pop and smiled at her squeak. "Like you fucking waited."

"Hell no." TJ moved closer and turned Chris's face with his fingers on her chin. He kissed her, coaxing her tongue to play with his.

Jon's cock jumped. Watching TJ make love to whatever woman they'd happened to be sharing at the time was a major turn on. Knowing they were bringing her to pleasure over and over again by doubling the sensations she felt was a high unlike any other. With Chris the emotions were magnified.

She evoked feelings in him he didn't know he had. She made him think of porch swings and watching the sunset together, of putting down actual roots. Now they just had to show her what they wanted and convince her that letting a man close wasn't always bad. Or men, in their case, since both he and TJ wanted the same thing with her—forever.

"You fucking taste so good, baby. Here and here." TJ's hand delved between them, pushing Jon's cock out of the way to cover her mound. "Let Jon take you, baby. I want to watch him push inside you. I want to watch you come around his cock."

Her head jerked back and thudded on the wall. White teeth came out to nibble on her lip and her body quivered with anxiety. Chris nodded. Jon and TJ gave a collective sigh of relief. If she had said no, Jon would have put her on her feet and backed off.

Thank God he didn't have to. He lifted her the few inches it took to lodge the head of his cock in her vagina. The rubber kept him from feeling everything he wanted—the wet heat of her outer lips sliding against him. All in due time.

He watched as she took inch by agonizing inch of his cock. She was tight as a fist around him, sucking him into her depths, milking him with muscles she squeezed as he penetrated.

"Fuck." He panted, caught between ramming into her and taking it slow.

"God, don't stop," she cried, jerking her head back and forth on the wall.

TJ flicked at one of her nipples then rolled it between his

thumb and forefinger. She moaned and arched into his touch. The action impaled her on Jon's cock, drawing a low growl from him.

Heaven on fucking Earth. He'd never get enough of her. He retreated and she gasped, bearing down with her pussy and trying to suck him back in. Still holding her hands above her head, he pressed back home. His balls tightened impossibly, threatening to spill their contents with those two simple strokes.

TJ's head lowered and he placed a simple kiss on the nipple he'd tormented with his fingers. His tongue flicked out, lapping at the brown-pink tip of her small breast before his lips closed around it. Chris's shoulders shot off the wall.

He didn't even have to move. With TJ working on her breasts, making her squirm, she was doing all the work for him. She pulled on his length as her hips shifted in time with the tugging at her nipples.

"Christ, you feel so good." He thrust into her, slapping her back against the wall, no longer able to control himself.

"More." Her head thrashed and she tried to tug her hands free with an anguished cry.

"Everything." Sweat beaded on Jon's forehead.

TJ's fingers slid along her belly, dipping into her navel and through the curls covering her mound to settle on her clit.

"Oh God." Chris's entire body stiffened and arched as TJ found the bundle of nerves at the top of her slit.

"That's it, baby." Jon felt TJ's knuckles rasp along his cock as he pushed in and out. Jon found the touch comforting. The first time it had happened had semi-shocked them both but then they'd both shrugged and continued pleasing the woman they'd been with. Now the coincidental touching didn't even faze them.

His balls drew up, signaling the impending eruption. Son of a bitch, he wanted to feel his come spurting into her with no protection. He'd never gone bareback before, never wanted to. Right now he'd give up everything he owned for the chance.

"Come for us, Chris." TJ's soothing demand seized her. She shattered, crying out and gripping Jon's hips with her legs in an unbreakable hold.

Jon felt every tiny ripple. It drew out his orgasm. He slammed into her one last time, burying his cock as deep as he could go. His neck corded as he threw his head back and growled with release. It went on and on, like no other orgasm he'd ever had.

Breathing hard and listening to TJ murmur inane things in her ear, Jon collapsed against her, supporting her with a cock that didn't understand it had just exploded with mind-blowing intensity.

Stupid thing wanted more. He wanted more. He wanted it all. His fingers loosened their hold on her wrists and they slipped from his hand to dangle at her sides.

"Oh my God."

TJ laughed. "We've reduced her to 'Oh my God'."

"Aislinn was so right." She swallowed and let her head drop back. "Can I take this off yet?" She tried to lift her hand to her face but lacked the energy and it fell useless, knocking against the wall.

TJ and Jon smiled at each other. They knew what she was talking about. Hell they'd overheard the conversation she'd had with Aislinn but they wanted to hear her say it. "What was Aislinn right about?" TJ asked.

"What?" This time she succeeded in removing the blindfold to stare at them with a perplexed look as if she didn't realize she'd spoken out loud.

"What was Aislinn right about?" TJ said softly again, encouraging her to talk to them.

She licked her lips. "Oh. Um. She, we... Nothing."

Jon didn't think it was possible for a face to get any redder. He pressed his hips forward, stroking her pussy until she moaned, and rubbed her cheek with his thumb. "Nothing my ass, sweetheart."

"We most certainly did not talk about your ass. Much, anyway."

TJ crossed his arms and sighed. Jon smiled again and, drawn to her still stiff nipples, pinched them lightly.

Chris sucked in a breath.

"As much as I like you talking about my ass with your friends, in this instance I don't think you were referring to my ass." He didn't know why it seemed so important to get her to admit she'd wanted to be with them.

She squirmed on his cock, hardening his flesh yet again and trying to distract him.

He wouldn't let her. Jon grabbed her hips and stilled her. "Don't even go there."

Chris lifted her lip in a semi-snarl before turning it into a pout.

TJ snorted. "That won't work either. We've got you pinned to the wall, literally, and neither of us plans on going anywhere until we're satisfied with the answer you give us. Talk."

The cheeks went pink again and she tucked her head to her chest. "Shetoldmetohaveaflingwithyou."

"What?" TJ lifted her face with a crooked finger under her chin. She blew out a breath that flapped her lips, stared at the ceiling as if it were the most interesting thing in the world and grudgingly spoke.

"She told me to have a fling with one of you. Well, no that's not really true, she said 'you' in general, as in both of you, and I thought she was crazy but obviously she was not and how many women have you done this with 'cause it really is kind of weird, not that I didn't like it because, wow, it was absolutely mind blowing and I really wouldn't mind doing it again—"

"Breathe," Jon barked. "Jesus. Ask a woman a simple question." He'd gotten what he'd wanted though, her admission that she wanted them. He wrapped his arms around her, hugging her to him. "My back is starting to kill me. Let's move this to the bed, shall we?"

Chris's gaze narrowed on him as she came to her senses. "Are you saying I'm fat?"

"Lord," TJ muttered, rolling his eyes. "What is it with you ladies?"

"Don't change the subject, Chris." Jon shifted her in his hold.

She yelped as he swung around and hobbled down the hallway to his bedroom with his cock still embedded in the sweet depths of her pussy and his pants falling off his waist. He opted for his room, knowing TJ's would be a mess, like always. The man had a strict aversion to making his bed and picking up his clothes despite being in the military, or perhaps because of it.

Chris squeezed his neck and hung on.

"My back hurts from banging you against the wall like an animal and then standing around while trying to follow your ramblings." He nipped at her ear, chuckling at the way she tried to scramble up his chest until she jerked at the sharp sound of a bark coming from behind the bathroom door.

"Eeee...put on the brakes, stop, back up the bus." She dug

her heels into Jon's ass and shot a hand out to catch the frame of the door they'd just passed, yanking them to a halt. Jon nearly stumbled. "What the hell was that?" Because it sure as shit sounded like a very familiar bark. Like that of her own German Shepherd. Which wasn't possible since he was safe and sound at her home.

Something niggled in her brain, something Aislinn had said about giving them her keys so they could get some stuff so she'd feel more comfortable. Nah. They wouldn't take her dog, would they?

"Sounded like a dog to me." TJ looked bored.

Chris gingerly pulled free of the thick penis which had minutes ago helped to give her a fantastic orgasm, a penis she was anxiously looking forward to getting to know better, along with another still hidden beneath the buttons of TJ's fly. For a second, her cheeks heated with the direction of her thoughts then she sobered.

After getting on her own feet she rested her fists on her hips, ignoring the fact she was nude from the waist up. "That's Clodhopper, isn't it? How the hell did my dog wind up here and why do you still have a penis?"

"Clodhopper," Jon muttered.

Her gaze shot to TJ's groin, since she knew for a fact Jon didn't have a problem with his equipment. The copious amount of moisture leaking onto her thighs was proof.

Her eyes widened just as TJ opened his mouth to speak.

"Oh my God. What did you do to my dog?"

TJ put his hands up in a soothing gesture. "Calm down. I didn't do anything. He's fine."

"Then how did you get him here? I know for damn sure he wouldn't have come willingly." She glanced again at his crotch, smiling when he covered it with both hands.

"Where the fuck did you learn to teach your dog to go for the balls?"

Chris smiled sweetly. Served him right for kidnapping her doggie.

This was what Aislinn had told them to bring from her house? She could cry right now. Aislinn knew Chris used Clod for protection, although fat lot of good he'd done her when her brother had shown up and Clod had been at the groomers. Had her brother waited for such a time? Had he been watching her? Didn't matter anymore. Besides, what better way to protect herself from these two men than a trained attack dog? She had to admit, having Clod here went a long way in making her feel safer though she was starting to believe she didn't need it. TJ and Jon weren't going to hurt her. Not physically anyway. They might break her heart when they were through with her, but she didn't think they'd cause her pain.

TJ grabbed her forearm when she reached for the door handle. Chris glanced down and grinned. "You might want to step back." His fingers flew off like she'd burned him. The second she opened the door, Clodhopper bounded out, tongue flapping, tail wagging.

"Shit."

"Motherfucker."

She felt the air move as both men jumped back.

"Hello, baby." Chris dropped to her knees and buried her head next to his. He panted and whined his greeting, his big paws landing on her thighs. His snout lifted, sniffing the air and looking over her shoulder at TJ and Jon. His lips curled and a low growl emanated from his chest.

"That's my good boy. He's very protective," she said over her shoulder.

"No shit, Sherlock." TJ pressed himself against the wall.

"And you call yourself a SEAL?" Chris rubbed the scruff of Clod's neck once more before standing. The feel of his fur tickling her naked breasts was more than a little weird.

"Do you see a gun in my hand right now? That dog nearly took off my manhood."

"Your *manhood*? I think they call that purple prose in fiction. Can I have my shirt back?"

"No."

The emphatic no came from both of them. Clodhopper took exception, snapping at the one closest to him, Jon.

He didn't seem the least bit impressed. "Call Cloddy off, Chris, and let's get back to the reason you're here, which we all now know has nothing to do with just a fling."

"But—"

"No buts. Call him off."

Jon didn't move from his perch, TJ didn't either, both of them presenting non-threatening positions.

"Oh fine, but just for the record, I really think it sucks that you broke into my house and stole my dog."

TJ was quick to answer. "I didn't break into your house, I had a key, and I didn't steal your beast, I brought him here so you would be more comfortable armed with the knowledge that if either of us did anything you didn't like, you could sic him on us."

She paused. A lump formed in her throat. Men weren't supposed to be thoughtful. They were supposed to use women and toss them away, not provide the protection against them.

"Clodhopper, at ease," she commanded, using the hand signal Clod would recognize. He immediately sat at her heel and panted, waiting for his next instruction. He wouldn't attack unless he felt Chris was being threatened or she gave him the command to attack. He'd do it without qualm, friend or not.

Jon straightened, stripped off the used condom as if that were the most important thing right now, then stuck his free hand out for Clodhopper to sniff, letting her dog get to know him.

"Why exactly did you give him a name like Clodhopper?" TJ joined Jon, a tad slower in offering his fingers to the wet nose and tongue of her dog. She could just imagine what had happened at her house.

"Because he had such big feet as a puppy. You drugged him, didn't you? That's why you still have your package?"

Jon stepped around her into the bathroom and disposed of the condom.

TJ nodded. "Didn't hurt him a bit."

"Next time I shoot you with a dart, I'll be sure and ask if it didn't hurt a bit," she grunted.

"Speaking of packages..." TJ adjusted himself. "Perhaps it's time we move this party into the bedroom." He stepped closer, invading her personal space and wrapping his scent around her. Her mouth watered, and her pussy flared to life. It appeared the niceties were through. She nodded and watched Jon's hand wrap around his cock and give a long, slow stroke.

Chris swallowed as a drop of pre-come leaked from the tip.

Each of them grabbed one of her elbows and tugged her to an open door at the end of the hall. The door shut with a resounding click, shutting Clodhopper out and making her jump with its implication. No escape. Did she even want to?

TJ stepped up behind her and hooked his thumbs in the elastic waistband of her skirt. He shimmied it over her hips to let it puddle on the floor. "We've been waiting too long for this to be just a one-nighter." He knelt and his hands wandered up from the backs of her knees to her butt cheeks, caressing and smoothing over the skin.

The up-close-and-personal attention her ass was getting embarrassed her, but she had a feeling there were far more exciting things about to happen than him touching her butt.

He proved it by spreading her cheeks and running his thumb the length of her crack, pausing to circle her anus. She gasped and rose up on her tiptoes. Her clit throbbed, her nipples hardened and damned if Jon wasn't drooling as he stared at the front of her body on display for him.

If she were at all self-conscious about her body, she might feel more awkward. As it was, she felt cherished, as if she were the only female on the planet who'd ever turned them on. She wasn't, but it was the way they both made her feel in this moment that mattered.

Jon's cock stood proudly from the juncture of his thighs. He wiggled out of the jeans hanging loosely on his hips and kicked them off, then stripped his black T-shirt over his head to reveal broad shoulders and abs thick with muscles that tapered into slim hips and firm thighs. He was covered in the perfect amount of hair. Not too much, not shaved like a swimmer.

TJ's hands moved up the small of her back, making her shiver, then to her front where they covered her breasts and plucked at her nipples. She glanced down, amazed at how big his hands were on her, how his tanned skin contrasted with her pale chest. His fingers were slightly rough—calloused, she guessed—and rasped at the sensitive buds exquisitely. She'd never stopped to think about how they would feel if a man ever really touched them.

One of her previous boyfriends had fondled them, but not *loved* them. Not shown them the attention TJ knew exactly how to show them. They weren't small, certainly not big either, but seemed to fit perfectly in the cup of his palms. He rolled the nubs in his fingers and she sucked in a breath. Between his touch and seeing Jon in the buff, she was more than ready for round two.

"Get on your hands and knees." TJ's lips roved over her ear, sending goose bumps down her arms.

For a woman who'd never had sex any way other than the missionary position, she was certainly receiving an education tonight.

Hell, she was having sex with two men in their home where they'd planned an entire seduction for her and were demanding she get on all fours. No biggie. She mentally snorted and wondered why in the hell she wasn't running for the front door, naked or not.

She gave the room a quick glance as she knelt on the floor, because for some reason she deemed it prudent to at least see where she was. Totally masculine in its furnishing, the room was done in dark blues and greens. A huge four-poster bed dominated the middle and a sudden panic flared to life. *They promised not to tie you down.* And Aislinn knew she was here, right?

A hand between her shoulder blades pushed gently, guiding her to put her palms on the floor. Chris hung her head. She wanted to think it was in shame, but the reality was, she wanted whatever was about to happen. Gravity pulled her breasts downward, the nipples drawn up tight.

There was a rustle of clothes behind her. TJ getting naked she hoped. Christ, they must have drugged her along with her dog. Just this morning she'd told TJ to get the hell away from her desk and here she was practically begging him to fuck her from behind.

She had to be dreaming. It was the only logical explanation for her plunge off the deep end.

"So soft." Lips whispered across the skin near her buttocks and she lifted her head. A pair of knees suddenly filled her vision. Her breasts swayed with her heavy breathing and her anticipation.

TJ moved, straddling her legs on his knees and tickling her calves and thighs with his hairier legs. His cock prodded her, first bumping into one butt cheek then hitting upon her slit. He separated her ass with his thumbs and his gaze bore into her like a one-ton weight.

She whimpered and dropped her head back down. How could she be doing this?

One hand left and she bit her lip. Surely he didn't think to do anything to her ass. Not tonight. Something cold plopped onto the tight pucker.

"Oh God."

"Relax, baby. If you don't like it, I'll back off, simple as that."

"Uhnnn..."

TJ's thumb pressed through the cold lubricant and she tensed. Jon sat in front of her, his erection at a furious angle right in front of her face. Fascinated by the pearly drop of come on the fat head, she relaxed, curving her spine and releasing the tension in her butt.

Jon's hand tangled in her hair, lifting the strands away so he could see her face.

"You ever done this before?"

She burst out laughing. "Which part? The going down on my hands and knees, the two men at once, letting someone stick their thumb in my ass, or the blow job I think is staring me in the face?" She glanced up at him. "You've got to be kidding, right?"

His smile said he liked her answer. His words cemented it. "I love your feistiness. I am specifically referring to the blow job, as you so eloquently put it."

She would have answered except at that moment TJ slid a finger into the one place on her body nothing had ever entered before. It hurt, yet felt good at the same time. She groaned and backed into him. He steadied her with the hand on her back again, pushing her forward until he had her where he wanted her, and pulled his finger nearly all the way out.

"Fuck, she's tight."

"Well duh," she wanted to shout but didn't. She wiggled, looking for more. "Since nothing's ever been..." He pushed in again. "Fudge." Chris collapsed onto her elbows and dropped her head on her forearm.

"What was that?" TJ asked, retreating and thrusting over and over, opening her up to what she was sure would be a bigger invasion sooner rather than later.

"Nothing," she snapped and heard TJ chuckle. Jon tilted her head and scooted closer. His penis would have poked her in the eye had she not yanked her head back some more.

And there it was again, in all its way-more-inches-than-she-could-handle glory. She realized she wanted to though. She wanted to take all she could of his length in her mouth and please him. It was the thought of swallowing what came out of said penis that made her pause.

Did everyone swallow? Did Jon expect her to? Would he be angry if she didn't? Christ, just thinking about it had her sweating and gagging. Fear of the unknown. Maybe it wouldn't be as bad as she was making it out to be. She agonized over the problem for precious seconds before deciding if he didn't like her not wanting to receive his come, then he could bite her. They'd essentially kidnapped her. If they made her do anything she didn't want, she considered that rape.

His cock waved before her eyes, begging her for some attention, and she swallowed.

"Hey." Jon's hands slipped around her cheeks and he looked into her eyes. "You don't have to do this."

Oh shit. He was going to make her cry. Again. She wasn't prepared for the tenderness. She had not been brought up to perceive men the way he was acting.

"I want to," she replied with steely determination. And she did. For him. For being a man she hadn't realized existed.

TJ added a second finger and she yelped as he widened the expanse of her exit. It couldn't be called an entrance. She didn't think God had really meant for it to be used as an entrance when he created it, but maybe he should have because holy shit, there was something to this whole back-door thing.

Then Jon's hands guided her head down and closer to the head of his erection and she decided she really wanted to know what he tasted like. With the flat of her tongue, she swiped at the velvet-soft skin and listened to him hiss.

Jesus, she was beautiful. Smooth, silky skin that pinkened whenever they touched her. Her juices literally dripped from her pussy, inviting TJ to lap at her again. First he had to work the rosy, puckered hole back there. She was fucking tighter than hell and his dick wanted in. Now.

He watched her head descend on Jon's cock, her mouth opening wide to take him in, and he could almost feel her lips wrap around his own erection. TJ groaned and fisted his cock with his free hand and continued twisting and penetrating her asshole with two fingers of his other hand.

Her body shuddered, her vaginal muscles contracted and released, giving him a peek into her pussy.

"Fuck it," he gritted out and leaned over her to reach for the box of condoms he'd dumped on the floor earlier. The action impaled her farther on his fingers. She shrieked and her head shot up, eliciting a growl from Jon.

"Sorry, man." TJ stayed where he was, bent over Chris, the tip of his cock inadvertently embedded in her pussy.

"Uh-huh," Jon ground out. "Real fucking sorry."

Chris dropped her head with an "*Uhn*." Sheer willpower kept him from thrusting into the wet heat surrounding his cock. Sweat beaded on his forehead and upper lip, his hips flexed and one more inch was sheathed by her pussy.

"Ah fuck. You're killing me here, babe." He rested his cheek on her back.

"Yeah, I can see where this is all my fault." She panted and wiggled her ass on his groin.

"Stop unless you want me to take you without a rubber."

She froze. TJ withdrew his fingers from her ass, drawing a low moan from her. He planted both hands on the floor on either side of her and didn't move.

"I'm—I'm on the pill," she offered, her lips grazing Jon's cock, her tongue flicking out along the vein running the length underneath.

"Shit. Don't say that." TJ couldn't help but push his hips forward another inch.

Her lips covered Jon's cock, her cheeks hollowed out as she sucked on him, then she released him with a pop before looking back at TJ. "I'm on the pill." Her eyes glittered with the same ferocious need he felt and he snapped.

TJ reared up on his knees and drove into her until his balls slapped against her clit. Chris arched back, mewling like a wildcat and squeezing his cock in a vise.

He wouldn't last a second. TJ gripped Chris's hips as she lowered her mouth again, causing Jon's head to fall back in ecstasy.

Then he was lost in the pounding of flesh on flesh, the wet slurp of his cock in her juices, of her mouth on Jon's penis, the drag and tug on his length and the constant whimpers and moans coming from both Chris and Jon.

The electricity between them sizzled. He met Jon's eyes over her shoulder and knew with one hundred percent certainty they had made the right choice in waiting for her. She made them whole. Jon nodded and with one last thrust, TJ erupted, letting the sweet depths of Chris's pussy catch every spurt of his come.

On and on it pulsed, unlike any other orgasm he'd ever had. Before he could catch his breath Jon gave a guttural warning and Chris sat back on her haunches. Her hand shot out to encircle Jon's cock and pumped twice. Thick, white streams of come shot from his tip to splash on his belly and her arm.

"I'm sorry," she whispered, suddenly going shy on them when it was all over.

TJ reached out and drew the hair back from her face. "Sorry you fucked us both?" He couldn't keep the incredulity from creeping out.

She waved him off with one hand and wiped her sweaty face with the other. "For not...you know."

Jon smiled and pulled her into his chest and therefore off TJ's cock. A position he sorely missed.

"For not what? Say the words, Chris." Jon kissed her lips and TJ sat back against the edge of the bed, sated, yet wanting to go again.

"Swallowing."

Jon tilted her face up to his. "I will never make you do anything you're not comfortable with. Let's get that out in the open right now. There are lots of women who don't like swallowing."

"So if I said I didn't like the whole sucking thing at all...?"

"I'd say based on the enthusiasm you showed by practically taking the skin off my cock, you're full of shit."

Her cheeks grew red and puffed out in exasperation. She tucked her head under Jon's chin. "I can't believe I just did that."

TJ did a double take. "You've never?"

"Well yeah." She buried her sheepish answer in Jon's chest as he idly rubbed a hand up and down her naked back. "Then I told myself I'd never do it again."

"So what made you change your mind?" Jon mumbled, his fingers wandering to an exposed nipple and tugging on it until she shivered.

"I have no idea." She huffed and turned into the touch. "I think you put a spell on me." Her eyelids slid closed and the tip of her tongue poked out to lick her bottom lip.

TJ made to stand. "More like your body knows who it can trust even if your brain doesn't." He scooped her up, loving the slight weight of her in his arms.

Jon rose to pull the comforter from his bed and TJ deposited her on the sheet he'd exposed. He bent over and teased her lips, coercing her to open and accept his tongue. One knee on the bed, he helped her scoot into the middle and then lay down next to her.

After a quick trip to the restroom, Jon joined them on the other side, effectively spooning Chris between them. TJ briefly thought about getting them into the shower, but by the way Chris appeared to be losing steam, he opted for staying in bed.

"I should have taken Aislinn's advice a long time ago," she murmured, yawning.

Jon propped himself on an elbow. "Yes, I think you should have," he teased.

She smiled, warming TJ's chest. TJ loved watching her smile. "I agree. You should take Aislinn's advice from now on when it comes to us."

She snorted. "We don't just talk about you guys. We talk about men in general." Her eyes flew open as if she realized what she'd said. "Damn." She flipped to her stomach and nestled her face in the pillow.

"Uh-uh." TJ rolled her back, a fierce possessive streak taking over. He didn't want to even think about her with another man touching all this exquisite skin or penetrating her sheath. She belonged to him and Jon now.

"I'll give you something to talk about the next time you chat with your girlfriend," Jon growled. He lifted her thigh over his and delved into her pussy with two fingers without preamble. His thumb circled her clit.

Chris arched her back and hissed at the contact. She reached behind her and gripped his ass with her fingernails to anchor herself. TJ went for the nipple closest to his mouth and sucked it deep into his mouth.

"Shit." She thrashed between them, unable to prevent the sensual attack to her body.

Within minutes they'd brought her to a quick peak and threw her over the edge. She gasped for breath as TJ flicked at her turgid nipple and Jon's fingers slowed in her pussy.

"Oh my God." She sank, boneless, into the mattress. "No

more. Mercy. White flag. I surrender."

"The surrender I'll take. There is no mercy though," TJ whispered in her ear. "You're ours. You can forget about all those other men."

She snorted. "What other men?"

"Exactly."

Jon drew the sheet over the three of them and he and TJ both wrapped an arm around the woman meant to be theirs.

Chapter Four

“What the fuck?” Jon glared at the red numbers on his clock. Three thirty-four. He’d only gotten about an hour’s sleep since their last go-round. What had woken him?

There. Music—bells—something ringing. Not close, so where the hell was it coming from? He glanced at Christina, dead asleep and snuggled up next to TJ. He was awake and staring back at him in confusion as well.

“What is that?” he whispered, careful not to wake their lover.

Jon looked at TJ. “She bring her cell in?” He stood and headed for the door.

“Not in hand. I think she had it in her pocket, didn’t she?”

By the time Jon found the skirt, the damn phone had stopped ringing. He grabbed it from the outer pocket. Anyone calling at three thirty in the morning didn’t want to chat. Maybe it was Aislinn, making sure she was okay, though why she would do that, he couldn’t fathom. Kyle wouldn’t have let her not trust them anyway.

The Caller ID screen displayed “1 Message”. Should he wake her? He stumbled to the bathroom to take a leak before climbing back into bed with the woman of his dreams and his best friend. The second his knee hit the bed, the phone jangled in his hand, screaming its ring now that it was out in the open instead of hidden in the folds of fabric.

Christina bolted upright and stared straight ahead. Her head swiveled from side to side, taking in her surroundings. The phone rang again and her head whipped toward his hand.

She snatched it from him. "You scared the hell out of me." Her hair fell in disarray around her beautiful face, tangled from being taken three times in the past five hours, and she clutched the sheet over her breasts.

Jon snorted as she flipped open the phone. "That sheet won't save you, baby." He gave it a tug and she stuck her tongue out at him.

"Hello?" Her voice cracked with sleepiness.

Jon stroked his hands over her naked back, and TJ did the same as she sat between them. She shivered between them and hugged her knees to her chest. Her breasts flattened against her thighs. Jon reached in and lifted the one closest to him.

"What?" Her voice whispered in eerie intonation, her knees fell to the bed, her hand shook. "No."

The strangled desperation Jon heard in her voice baffled him. TJ sensed the same thing. He sat up, tucking her into the V of his thighs, and ran his fingers through her hair. The look he gave Jon asked the question he wanted to know too. *What the hell had happened?*

"When?" Tears filled her eyes and spilled over the lower lids. She sniffed and wiped her nose with the back of her hand.

"What's goin' on, baby?" TJ demanded.

"How did this happen?" she shouted, making both of them jump.

"Oh God." Her wail cut into his heart. The phone slipped from her ear and landed with a soft thud on the mattress between her legs. Chris leaned into TJ with a soulful keening sound.

Jon picked up the phone, anger roiling through him at whoever had upset their woman.

"Shh," TJ consoled.

The line was dead. Motherfucker. What had he done by bringing the damn thing into their bed?

"Talk to us, sugar." TJ's words seemed to echo in the thick atmosphere of the room.

"He killed her."

Oh God, he'd done it. After all this time, her father had finally succeeded in going too far and now her mother was dead. Her heart split in two. If it weren't for the constant touch of TJ's fingers grounding her, she might have lost it. More so than she'd already done.

It couldn't be true. Her aunt had to be wrong, misled somehow. Maybe her mother was unconscious, hurt like every time before but not dead. She couldn't be dead. Oh God, oh God, oh God. She hummed and felt her body sway. Her stomach lurched.

"Christina." Jon's sharp voice jerked her back.

She searched his face, seeing the worry lining his eyes, the bunching of his jaw.

"What happened?" he asked, reaching up to flip a lock of hair that covered her eye.

"He killed my mother." She nearly choked on the words. Somehow she'd known, deep in her subconscious, this day would come. She just hadn't expected it would be this soon.

TJ turned her face to his with a finger under her chin. Tears threatened to spill. She could hardly hold them back and didn't want to. Let them see her in all her glory. If they couldn't handle this then she would know once and for all that tonight really had been a fling for them, despite what they'd said earlier.

A small amount of light illuminated the room. Since she didn't believe for a minute either one of them slept with a light on, she could only think they'd left it on in deference to her being there. She was grateful for it. Those kinds of little things were the ones that made all the difference, made her feel special and not just like the next woman in a lineup of women.

"Who did?" TJ growled.

Shit. For a second it had gone away. "My father," Chris breathed.

How many times had she watched him beat her mother, only to wake up the next morning begging for forgiveness for what he'd done? How many times had her mother accepted those pathetic excuses and apologies? Despite the love she had for her mother, she was just one of the reasons Chris had had to leave. Watching your mother deny day after day the problem so obviously staring her in the face had torn Chris apart.

"What do you know, Chris? Who was on the phone?"

"My aunt." She shook her head, dispelling the image of her mother laying motionless at the bottom of the staircase leading to the second floor of the home she'd grown up in. "They found her at the...the foot...of the stairs." She sobbed and turned into TJ's chest. His arms wrapped her in a warmth she'd never felt before. At her back, Jon added his extra strength. Who'd have thought she'd ever find herself seeking comfort from one man, let alone two? Still, even sandwiched between the two men who'd shown her so much pleasure throughout the night, her skin was cold and clammy.

"I know he did it." Her mother may have been many things

Chris never wished to be, but clumsy or suicidal weren't two of them.

"What do the police say?" Jon tried to warm her by rubbing her arms, TJ started in on her legs. The shaking began almost immediately, racking her body with enough force to make her teeth ache.

"I don't know." What could they say? What had they ever said when she'd called them? *There's nothing we can do until your mother files charges.* Stupid!

She sniffed and felt the claustrophobia setting in. She couldn't move, couldn't breathe. "I...I have to go. I have to be with her. She's all alone." Chris fought her way out of their embrace, irrational thoughts clouding her mind.

"No fucking way. You can fight us 'til you're blue in the face, but no goddamn way are you going there alone," Jon snarled.

She gasped and spun to face the vehement face he presented.

"Don't even think about it. We'll get up, take a shower, get dressed and then we'll get underway."

"Listen to him, baby. No matter what you thought would happen tonight with us, we aren't ready to let you go." TJ's lips caressed the back of her neck. "We're here for you. Don't shut us out."

She couldn't handle this right now. A fling. A fling was what she'd been semi-prepared for, not shoving her sordid life down their throats and having them accept her, flaws and all. Her heart pounded against her ribs. Her brain screamed not to put her faith in them, but her body demanded she do the opposite. It all boiled down to trust, because trusting them not only affected her mind, but her heart.

The last thing she wanted was for them to stomp all over

her when they were ready to move on, leaving her in tatters the way her father had done too many times to count.

Chapter Five

What exactly was it with the clichéd funeral in the rain? Chris stared at her mother's casket. The flowers covering the silver box were beautiful, so unlike the life she'd led, one fraught with turmoil with a man she refused to stop loving no matter how many times he belittled her or beat her.

Chris shivered. The rain had put a chill in the air. Then again, it could be the two men still standing at her back, their mere presence lending strength. The small gathering who'd come to Lana Marshall's final resting place had long since disbanded but Chris could not find the strength to move. Yet not once had TJ or Jon tried to get her to. Each had a hand on her shoulders where their fingers gave her a continual massage.

She should be crying. She should be bawling uncontrollably and asking God why He'd allowed this. Would it help? No. God hadn't killed her mother. Maybe He'd saved her instead since she hadn't seemed able to save herself.

Chris had cut all ties to her father a few years ago, but in doing so she'd been severed from her mother as well. Not so her younger brother. Somehow she must have done all her crying in the past and over the last couple of days because now she was dry.

She sucked in a breath and held it, inhaling the smells of the rain and the fresh flowers and the damp earth her mother would be lowered into as soon as she moved away. Off to her left, trying to be discreet, were two men dressed in grey jumpsuits waiting for her to leave so they could do their job.

Jon's hand sifted through her hair and she dropped her shoulders.

"You okay, baby?" TJ's lips caught on her ear.

She nodded. "Yes."

He came to the front and kneeled before her, taking her hands in his. "Is there anything we can do for you?"

"No." She gave a short laugh. "You've already done way too much."

Jon sat in the chair next to her. "We haven't done anything."

"Are you kidding me? You brought me all the way out here, in your personal airplane no less, listened to me cry for hours on end and came to a funeral for a woman you've never met. You call that doing nothing?"

Jon's lips quirked into a smile. It made her tummy flip and sent an arrow of hunger to her clit. She jerked her gaze away only to have it fall on TJ, whose face mirrored Jon's. She should not be feeling like this right now. Not in the midst of burying her mother. Yet the hardening of her nipples told her that her body didn't care where the hell she was.

"What's next, baby?" TJ put a hand on her bare knee. His thumb caressed her skin and she had to swallow and lick her lips to keep herself from tackling him to the ground.

This is wrong. It took a Herculean effort but Chris managed to push his hand off.

One of his eyebrows rose. "Too much help in taking your mind off things?"

"I'm supposed to be in mourning," she murmured.

Jon's lips brushed her ear. "I don't think you have any tears left in you, sugar. No one can say you haven't done any mourning."

"It just doesn't seem right to be sitting here thinking about anything other than the fact that my mother is dead."

TJ sighed. "No one is judging you, sweetheart. Everyone grieves in their own way at their own pace."

She sniffed and nodded. He was right but it still felt wrong. Like she was betraying her own mother. "She always chose my father over my brother and me. I never understood why she liked getting the shit kicked out of her. Still, she is...was my mother. She gave birth to me and at least had some input in raising me." So why couldn't she drum up more sympathy?

"You want to go home?" Jon settled his hand on the back of her neck and massaged.

Yes. "No." She couldn't just leave. Not without going to the house to be there for her brother one last time before she left for good. The only reason she would ever come home was gone now.

Carter would be there and she'd have to deal with his pathetic attempts at demanding she loan him money to support his habit. He was as big as their dad and just as ugly with his alcohol.

Maybe she shouldn't go to the house. It might be safer, body and mind, to leave and never look back.

"No. No, I need to do this. I need to say goodbye."

Jon nodded and slapped his thighs before he stood and they both helped her up.

"Then let's get it over with so we can get back home." TJ wrapped her long hair in his hand and brushed his lips against hers.

He tasted so good. Jon pressed himself along her back. His erection prodded her bottom and she whimpered in need. How long had it been since she felt their cocks inside her? Two days? Her brain was completely befuddled. The last she really remembered was waking up in Jon's bed with the initial phone call from her aunt.

Somewhere over the next couple of days they'd flown her home to the Chicago suburb she'd grown up in and spoken to the police to try to piece together what had happened the night her mother died.

She'd basically gotten the runaround. No one knew anything. No one saw anything. As far as they were concerned Carter found her already dead at the bottom of the stairs when he came home from work and her father had been at work all day. So at some point between eight in the morning and four in the afternoon, Lana Marshall had fallen down the stairs and broken her neck.

TJ reached for the handle of the door to their rental car. She didn't even remember walking across the expansive cemetery grounds to get there but suddenly she was standing in the wedge created by the open back door.

A fling. Aislinn had told her to have a fling. She had to laugh.

"What's this all about, sugar?" Jon wiped a tear from her face when her laughter finally subsided.

She smiled. TJ had her blocked in. She wasn't going anywhere yet again. Talk about déjà vu. The only thing that would make this scenario any more similar would be the dimness of late evening. Oh, and a silky black blindfold.

Chris cocked her head. "Does this look familiar?"

Jon glanced around at the three of them and grinned. "Why yes, madam, it does." He leaned closer and nuzzled her nose with his. "And here's me without my blindfold." His low grumble coursed through her, filling her clit with blood and making it ache to be touched.

"It was just supposed to be a fling." She groaned.

TJ cleared his throat. "We'll be sure to take the matter up with Aislinn as soon as we get home."

"Home sounds nice," she whispered, tilting her head to take Jon's lips. He opened, sucking her tongue into his mouth, and took control of the kiss.

"Our home," TJ added.

Panting, Chris broke off and licked her lips, tasting Jon there. She faced TJ and her knees wobbled. It hit her like a two by four to the face. *Our home* sounded better than anything she'd ever heard before. She knew with sudden certainty that she definitely wanted more than a fling too.

She'd take whatever she could get, for as long as they wanted her, and deal with the aftermath of them leaving her when it happened.

First she had to get through the next few grueling hours in the presence of her condescending family and friends who didn't understand how she could move away and never come back.

She'd seen the faces of the people at the funeral. The raised eyebrows, the lips curled in distaste, the whispering with not even an attempt at being behind her back. Under normal circumstances she would have had a panic attack. She would have let their hatred wash through her to the point she couldn't breathe, couldn't move.

Instead, TJ and Jon had never left her side. Hell, there wasn't a moment when at least one of them didn't have a hand on her. They had effectively grounded her and kept the attacks she'd suffered her entire life at bay.

"I'd like that. Very much."

TJ's nostrils flared with her declaration and his lips melded with hers. When he finally lifted away, he pushed her hair behind an ear. "You don't know how good that makes us feel. Let's get this over with and get back on the plane."

ಌ

All talk stopped the second she came through the door. The eerie silence filled the living room of the house she'd grown up in, sending a chill over her body and leaving goose bumps along her bare arms. Every eye in the room was on her. Talk about being the life of the party.

Except this wasn't a party. It was her mother's memorial. Surely they didn't think she wouldn't show up? TJ stepped in behind her and ushered her forward with a hand at her back. Jon followed.

The airplane suddenly looked better and better. Why had she talked herself into this?

"Come on, baby. Pay your respects and don't worry about these people." TJ clasped her fingers through his and tugged her deeper into the room.

Some kind of ballgame played on the years-old TV, and people she used to call friends huddled on the threadbare sofa, loveseat and chairs, whispering and glaring as if she'd committed a crime. If only they knew the life she'd really lived behind closed doors.

Hell, they did know, they just hadn't cared. All those people staring goggle-eyed at her right now were adults she'd trusted. They should have protected her. Instead, they'd turned a blind eye. Maybe they were the biggest reason she'd run the second she'd gotten the chance.

It takes a village to raise a child...

Where had her village been?

"Just let me find my father and brother and then we can leave," she murmured. It was plain to see there was nothing left for her here. Even the deputy sheriff, Blake Anderson, who stood off in one corner, turned his head when she looked at him. At least he had the decency to look ashamed by the behavior in the room.

"I think I saw 'em in the kitchen," someone snarled.

Chris did her best to ignore the attitude for which she'd done nothing to deserve. She straightened her shoulders, lifted her chin and headed for the booming sound of her sloshed father.

Some memorial this was for a woman who shouldn't have had to give her life to the man who beat her every night.

Jon pushed through the swinging door and they were greeted by the same reaction they'd had in the living room. Dead silence.

Her father's lip curled up in distaste when he saw her. He took a long swig of the half-empty beer bottle he held, wiped his mouth with the back of his hand, belched and then tossed the bottle in the air, flipping it end over end. He caught it upside down by the neck and threw it in Chris's direction like he was throwing a hatchet.

Everything happened at once. She screamed, TJ yanked her toward his chest, covering her head with his hands, and Jon launched himself across the room at Robert Marshall with a primal yell. The glass bottle shattered against the wall and tinkled to the ground.

Her brother, Carter, stomped across the kitchen, ignoring

Jon, who subdued her father with minimal effort against the sink, one arm thrust up and back behind him. Robert howled in pain, screeching for Jon to get the fuck off him.

The door flew open. Deputy Anderson had one hand on his gun and probably ten looky-loos behind him.

"What the fuck are you doing here?" Carter roared at Chris, raising a hand to slap her.

Chris cowered.

She didn't need to. TJ grabbed Carter's hand before it had the chance to make its sweep and bent it backward, bringing Carter to his knees.

"You better get some handcuffs out, Deputy, or I can't guarantee I won't break this arm." TJ's expression was one she'd never seen on him before. Feral might best describe it. Yet his words were calm.

"She fucking killed her." Carter's howl was punctuated by a vicious bend to his arm and a yelp of pain.

Deputy Anderson took his time retrieving the cuffs at his belt. There was something on his face. Almost a look of...satisfaction? Shock held her immobile.

"How can you accuse *me* of this?" She expected the rejection, even hatred or violence from her father—he probably felt the need to turn on someone since his punching bag was gone now, but not accusation, and certainly not from her brother. She hadn't even been there, for God's sake. The tears threatened to start up again.

"Kind of hard to kill someone from a state away," Jon threw over his shoulder.

She could see neither of her protectors had broken a sweat yet her brother was practically in tears on the floor.

"My mother hated her for leaving." Spittle shot from

Carter's mouth.

"Shut the fuck up, boy." Robert attempted to turn around only to have Jon jerk his arm higher. He gave a drunken hiss.

"If she had stayed, this wouldn't have happened." Carter's eyes bugged and sweat coated his face.

"What wouldn't have happened, Carter?" Deputy Anderson asked.

"She wouldn't have fallen down the fucking stairs, you moron. She was always moaning and wailing about that bitch." He stabbed a finger in Chris's direction.

A thousand thoughts went through her head, the topmost being what had she done? Had she killed her mother even if inadvertently?

Deputy Anderson stepped closer, admiring the hold TJ had on Carter, but still not attempting to handcuff her brother.

"I was so fucking sick of her pathetic whining. You'd think Christina was a princess the way she talked about her," Carter spat.

The tears fell. Her mother had loved her after all. She'd never said the words to her, or shown her with hugs, but for Carter to be spouting what he was, Lana had to have felt *something* for her only daughter.

"So what did you do?" the deputy asked, obviously looking for something. A confession, maybe?

"Nothing that we shouldn'ta done sooner," her father screamed.

Chris gasped as did the onlookers behind them all.

Anderson sighed as if he'd had enough and slipped the cuffs from his belt. He stepped around the stunned Carter and slapped one end on her father's wrist, bringing it out of Jon's hold. "Robert Marshall, you have the right to remain silent." He pulled both of Robert's arms behind his back and Chris heard the click of the second cuff.

She heard something about assault and battery but not much else over Carter shouting, "You can't fucking take him. That's entrapment. He didn't do anything but find that bitch dead."

A second later, three more deputies pushed through the mob at the door to help secure both her father and Carter and lead them through the house and outside.

Chris stood there stunned. What in the hell had just happened?

Deputy Anderson stopped in front of her as Jon once again took his place at her side and TJ the other. She warmed in an instant.

"I'm sorry, Christina. I didn't want for this to happen this way but we hadn't had any luck getting either one to crack. I figured you might be some kind of impetus."

"But what if I hadn't come?"

He shrugged. "Then I would have gotten them some other way. Besides, we haven't really gotten them yet. The coroner's report could only say she died in the fall. They couldn't prove if she was pushed or not, but, honey, I know how things went down in this house. She may have blamed her bruises and broken bones on being clumsy, but she wasn't. Your mama was a good woman in her own way, she just wasn't strong as you when it came to getting the hell out. There wasn't a true confession back there, but I'd had enough of their caterwauling, and they did attack you, so I had a reason to arrest them. Do you have a number where I can keep you informed? The minute I know anything, I'll let you know."

Jon handed the deputy his card. "We appreciate it."

Chapter Six

Chris sank into the buttery-soft leather seat of the jet and let sheer exhaustion take over. The last couple of hours had proven to be more hellish than the moment she'd learned of her mother's death. First they'd followed her father and brother to the police station and she'd listened in as her father continued to spout his evilness, never confessing so much as saying her mother had gotten what she'd had coming to her. His filth hurt worse than any physical blow he could have landed. And he still blamed Chris for her mother being so depressed that she'd probably taken her own life.

His ramblings had been so ridiculous—depressed after all these years, when all she had to do was call?—Chris had finally gotten up and walked out, but not before he'd turned his venomous filth on her, shouting and spitting and vowing vengeance through the one-way glass. For *what* she didn't know. She hadn't caused her mother to die. Robert Marshall was even more delusional than she remembered him being.

He hadn't once mentioned caring that his wife had lain at the foot of those stairs like some kind of animal until Carter had gotten home and found her. Hell, he hadn't shown any kind of remorse whatsoever in losing Lana.

Remembering the look he'd given Chris when she'd walked past him and out of his life for the second time made her nauseous still. Full of hatred, it alone promised retribution.

Chris wanted nothing more than to be home where she could snuggle under the covers and let it all go. She looked up the aisle to the two men who'd brought her here and scratched her idea. She wanted to be at *their* home, in *their* bed, wrapped in *their* arms, letting them take care of her. They'd proven to her through the stress of the funeral, the memorial and the police station they could be more than the sex machines she'd always envisioned them being. Didn't help that she'd listened to all the rumors about them.

The last couple of days should have scared them off her completely. She was a woman with more emotional baggage than a sea of women, any one of which they could have chosen instead of her. But they hadn't. Instead they'd insisted on coming with her. They'd held her hand and rubbed her shoulders and never once had she been left alone. They were a pillar of comfort at a time when she would have had no one. She would forever be grateful for that.

Chris glanced back up at Jon talking to the pilot and TJ to the steward. TJ gestured to the back room of the plane. It had been her intention to head there first thing, but she'd only made it to the second row of seats before collapsing.

Beyond the closed door was a big bed. For now it would have to suffice for snuggling under the covers. TJ's concern-filled gaze met hers. He walked away from the steward, leaving the other man talking to his back, and stopped a foot away from her. He lifted a hand, palm up. "Come on."

His gravelly voice sent a frisson of pleasure through her when there should be none. How did both of them do that to her so easily? It was like her body knew they owned it and would give in at the weakest suggestion, but nothing about his demeanor said he was suggesting anything. Her legs shook like wet noodles as she stood.

TJ lifted her hand to his mouth and kissed across her knuckles. Did he have any idea what he was doing to her, turning her inside-out? He pivoted and led her to the bedroom.

"Take off your clothes, baby, and lie down for awhile. Time to try and rest. You look like you're about to keel over."

She stared at him. He must have gone crazy. He'd asked her to get naked and into bed, then tacked on a "try and rest". She hadn't thought it possible for men to think of naked and rest in the same sentence. Her eyes watered. She'd gotten this same kind of reaction from them for two days. No fooling around, no insinuating sex, just seeing to her needs.

Chris sat on the edge of the king-sized bed and crazily wondered how they'd gotten the damn thing on the plane. It took up most of the space in the room, leaving just enough to open the door to the tiny lavatory on one side and nothing on the other.

TJ loosened the tie he'd worn for the funeral and pulled it from around his neck with a whoosh. His shoes were next. He toed the shiny loafers off at the heel, his gaze never leaving hers.

"Need help?" He smiled at her. Not the devilish, I-want-to-fuck-you smile she expected but a tender one that said he understood what she was going through and made her feel a hundred pounds lighter. Chris kicked off her own shoes, a pair of heels she rarely wore for a damn good reason—they scrunched her toes to oblivion—and jumped to her feet. Reaching beneath her skirt, she rolled the much-hated pantyhose down her legs and sat again to pull them off completely.

TJ had his belt unbuckled, his pants unbuttoned and unzipped, his shirt untucked, and was in the process of relieving himself of his shirt. It fell to the ground with a soft thud and he crossed his arms in front of his belly. His back arched as he lifted the undershirt up and over his head, tossing it to the floor also.

Chris's heart thudded. The sight of his ripped abs was absolutely mouth watering. She understood how he and Jon drew so many women to themselves. They were drool-worthy.

"Don't make me remind you one more time to strip, baby."

Shit. Chris shook her head, but nothing would divest her mind of the image before her—a sleek line of dark hair leading from his chest and disappearing into the top of his boxers.

One of TJ's eyebrows rose. Chris felt her face heat.

She flew off the bed again and fumbled with the button at the side of the skirt. Damn. Her fingers felt like sausages. In the end she simply yanked it down over her hips and cringed at the ripping she heard along the waistband. Why the hell was she so anxious to get out of her clothes?

"Oh good, you had the same idea." Jon's voice made her head snap up. A huge smile revealed his straight white teeth. She felt her cheeks heat and wondered if he'd heard her clothes rip in her eagerness to get them off her body.

"Yeah, well, I didn't think she'd do it unless I provided a little encouragement." TJ stepped over and pulled her against his chest. His lips feathered over hers, his hands held her gently at her hips.

She melted against him, letting him take her weight, and opened her mouth under his. Fling, schming. She'd been deluding herself thinking she wanted this relationship to end.

The idea should have shocked her. It didn't. She'd been a non-believer in men for so long, yet here she was falling for two of them, and if she were truly honest with herself, she'd have to say she'd been slowly headed this direction for months. Self-protection had held her back.

TJ's hands wandered under her blouse, carrying the fabric up as they went. "Hands up," he murmured.

She complied and let him rid her of the shirt, leaving her in only her panties since she hadn't worn a bra. The rasp of a zipper sounded next to her. She hadn't even realized Jon had moved, she was so focused on TJ and his kiss and touch. Now Jon turned them so he could stand behind her, his chest along her back. His hands covered her breasts and plucked lightly at her nipples, drawing a sigh from her.

This was right where she wanted to be.

Jon nibbled on her ear as the plane's engines whined to life. TJ's fingers trailed down her abdomen, pausing to swirl in her navel. Then his touch was gone and she felt a pat on her butt. "Get into bed, baby."

Chris hesitated and bit her lip before clearing her throat. "How?"

"How what?"

"How do you want me," she rasped, feeling heat coil deep in her belly.

TJ chuckled. "In the middle on your side."

She reached for the waistband of her panties. Jon stopped her. "Leave 'em on."

"Wha—?"

"You take them off and I'll want to do something you're not prepared for right now."

TJ rubbed his hands up and down her arms. "We're just sleeping, Chris. No sex. Sleep. You've had a hard couple of days and when we make love to you again, we want you whole, not pieces of yourself."

Tears filled her eyes. This was not how men were supposed to act. They were supposed to take, take, take. Yet TJ and Jon had shown her time and again just how opposite they were to men like her father and brother. She mouthed *thank you* to Jon, took a deep breath and stretched out on the bed. It tilted as TJ climbed on after her, then Jon. They sandwiched her, lending their warmth to her chilled skin and cocooning her in their dual embrace.

She'd never felt more protected or loved. Or less tired. Her exhaustion seemed to have disappeared in their arms and suddenly she wanted answers.

"Why do you do this?"

"What?" Jon's voice was groggy, indicating she wasn't the only one who'd been tired.

"Share."

TJ rubbed his nose in the crease of her shoulder. "It just sort of happened one night when we were with the SEALs. Made us both sit up and see how much we were missing, that we could feed off each other's excitement and make the woman feel that much better." His lips traveled across the back of her neck.

"It made finding a woman who enjoyed a ménage that much more special," Jon added, his fingers wandering over her belly. "Like you," he whispered. "We've been waiting for the one woman who would make us feel whole." His gaze met hers, making her breath catch. "We've been waiting for you."

TJ's arm slipped over her hip and his hand settled over her navel, big and strong and firm. And permanent. Chris swallowed as the irrevocable feeling fluttered in her tummy. More than she'd ever wanted something like this in the past, she wanted their offering of permanence now.

ଓଷ୍ଠ

The scenery from the airport to their house passed in a blur. Her head felt foggy, her legs like Jell-O and despite the nap, Chris felt like she could sleep for another whole day and still be tired.

Yet her body was practically bathed in their cologne, all thanks to the way they'd snuggled on the plane. Her fingers itched in her lap and twice she'd had to force the toes of her left foot to stop tapping. The fabric of her blouse rubbed incessantly on her nipples to the point she wanted to reach up and fondle them herself.

She took a deep breath and stared out the window, desperate for something to distract her from the two men occupying the car with her. The two men who'd lent her support when she needed it most. A time when she'd never imagined having such support, let alone that two men would be the ones providing it.

For so long she'd seen them as eye candy. She'd told herself—to save her sanity most of all—that they were men who flitted from one bimbo to the next seeking only the pleasure of their bodies and not their minds. God, she'd been such an idiot. The truth had been staring her in the face day in and day out and because she hadn't wanted to take a chance, she'd been too stupid to see how far from her perception Jon and TJ truly were.

They weren't in it for the sex. They were in it, in her, for a relationship. A long-lasting relationship, and if she hadn't taken that leap of faith the other night with TJ and Jon, she might still be stuck up in Chicago dealing with the ramifications of her father killing her mother instead of here with them sheltering her.

"Almost home, baby. You still tired?" TJ turned the BMW into the neighborhood lined with massive homes, century-old oaks and beautiful landscaping. In the light of day and without the heavy weight of her mother's death smashing her, she looked at the area with new eyes. Stunning was an apt word. The rich lived here and TJ and Jon had their fair share of wealth.

"Yes," she murmured. Except a part of her woke up with the way his voice made her body tingle. She squirmed in her seat. Jon reached over from his position beside her in the backseat and threaded his fingers through hers.

She'd been more than ready for them back on the plane. Hell, when she'd been stripping off her clothes it had felt like a race to see who would get done first. Instead they'd wrapped her in a man burrito and held her while she'd slept. They'd still been there when the plane had landed and she'd woken.

Would they put her off again? Because honestly, she didn't think she could handle being coddled. She wanted something to take her mind off everything that had happened in the last few days and hopefully they understood they could provide the something.

TJ pulled up to an all-brick, expansive ranch sitting on a huge tract of land she hadn't really seen yet. The first time she'd been here it had been getting dark and she'd been, well, blindfolded, and then they'd left in the wee morning hours when it had still been dark, first to drop off Clodhopper with Aislinn and Kyle and then on to her childhood home. Now, she was getting her first good look at TJ and Jon's home and she really liked what she saw. You could probably fit three houses between theirs and their neighbors' and still have room to spare. She envisioned a tiny little girl running across the lawn, laughing. Chris shook her head to dispel the thought. Children? She snorted.

"Problems?" Jon leaned into her and glanced out her window as if looking for whatever she found amusing.

"No, just glad to be home." She jerked around and faced him. It was now or never. "You won't...er, um, hold back will you?"

TJ brought the car to a stop. One of Jon's eyebrow's rose. "Hold back?"

Chris fidgeted. Why was it so hard to say what she wanted? "I don't want to be held." There. That ought to do it.

"You don't want to be held?" His words sounded hurt but his face held a touch of amusement. The rat was having a good time pretending not to understand her. She lunged at him, attacking his lips with her mouth and giving him no room for misunderstanding.

"Well, hell. I for one am extremely grateful there will be no holding involved." TJ shoved his door open and jumped out. Lips still locked on Jon's, Chris watched TJ from the corner of her eye as he jogged around the hood and came to her door. He flung it open and hauled her out with his hands under her armpits. Jon followed, barely breaking their contact.

She found herself shepherded toward the front door, pushed inside and thrust into a serious sense of déjà vu. She'd been in this spot before, that first night. This time they didn't stop inside the door but pushed her down the hall, kissing and touching her wherever they could reach along the way.

Everything fled her mind except being closer to her men. Just for these few minutes—or hours, whatever the case may be—she wanted to forget the ugliness her father had wrought and be free.

The bedroom was dim with the shades drawn but she saw everything clearly. They came to a stop in the middle of the room. Jon stepped up behind her, pressing his cock into the small of her back. TJ dropped to his knees in front of her, taking her skirt and panties with him, over her hips and down her legs.

"Step out." He tapped each knee and in the process, placed her feet where he wanted them, she guessed, because she ended up with her legs spread wide open.

Her knees threatened to buckle when TJ spread her labia with his thumbs and blew on the heated flesh.

Chris let her head fall back on Jon's chest and reached back to grip his hair. He chuckled in her ear, his fingers twirling and pinching the tips of her breasts beneath her shirt before stripping it up and over her head. Every ounce of her blood must have surged into her sex and nipples, as sensitive as they both were. TJ's tongue slid through her sopping wet folds with ease, from back to front, and ended at the tiny bulge of her clit. He circled the nub and sucked it into his mouth.

"Oh God." She started to sink to the ground only to be held up by Jon.

"Uh-uh, sugar. TJ's not done with you yet," Jon murmured, his tongue sliding into her ear canal. She bit her lip. She couldn't take much more and she was sure they'd just begun.

Again and again TJ lapped at her, slurping her cream and feasting on her. He'd never get enough of her. His cock was hard as a rock but he didn't dare touch it. He wanted to be buried inside this pretty little pussy before he exploded.

TJ wrapped his lips around her clit peeking out from beneath its hood and she shot to her toes. If Jon weren't holding her up, TJ was sure she'd have melted to the floor a long time ago.

He took one last swipe and stood, showering her belly and breasts with kisses on the way.

"Your body's all flushed, baby. Nice and wet and ready for us."

Chris licked her lips. He had a better place for that tongue of hers.

TJ palmed her right cheek. Her nostrils flared with each panting breath.

"I need to feel your mouth on my cock, baby. On your knees." He freed his erection from the confines of his pants and boxers and shoved both down to his knees.

For a split second her eyes widened. Then she swallowed and sank to the ground as if she'd done it a thousand times. He knew from the first night and her tentativeness at going down on Jon she hadn't. Still, when her lips wrapped around the head of his cock and drew on it, his eyes rolled back in his head and he nearly lost his balance.

Who needed experience when you had raw talent and enthusiasm?

"Shit," he growled when she swept over the bundle of nerves near the tip. Fuck, she seemed to know exactly where to touch, how hard to suck, how much to take in— "Uhn."

Jon grunted in laughter and stripped his clothes off. "Now you know."

TJ grasped her hair in his hands and held her still on his cock. Jesus. Thirty seconds in her hot mouth and he was ready to come. Obviously her tentativeness had gone by the wayside.

"No more," he groaned and pulled away. Shiny wet, his cock twitched in protest. TJ lifted his chin. "On the bed."

He smiled when she readily obeyed. Her ass wiggled as she climbed up and crawled across the bed, giving him a fantastic peek at the rosy aperture between firm cheeks. TJ nodded at Jon, who turned and grabbed a duffle bag from the floor near the foot of the bed.

Two steps later, TJ kicked his pants off and knelt on the bed behind her. Chris turned, a heated look on her face.

Her pussy glistened between her thighs, beckoning him in.

"Raise your leg, baby." TJ patted the thigh he wanted moved and slid beneath her so she straddled him. She gasped as his cock trailed a line of his pre-come across her hip and nudged the folds of her pussy.

"You're going to take me in both, aren't you?" There was a hint of fear in her words but her eyes held a touch of excitement. Her pulse hammered at the V of her neck. TJ tilted his head and placed a soft kiss there.

"I'm going to have help," he murmured and fingered her nipples. She arched her back like a kitten and purred.

TJ watched as Jon ran his hands over the globes of her ass. "Perfect."

Chris's forehead landed on TJ's chest. "Is this gonna hurt?"

Both he and Jon burst out laughing. God he loved her.

Stunned at the direction of his thoughts, TJ lifted Chris's head with his thumb under her chin.

"You will take us both and you will love it, baby."

Her eyes glittered. Jon held up a tube of lubricant and TJ gave a slight nod.

"What if I...don't?" she squealed when Jon's finger penetrated the tight ring of muscles of her ass.

TJ reached for her clit and circled it.

"Shit." Her head dropped and her body shook above him.

"You will."

"Relax, sugar, let me stretch you."

Chris whined but her hips pushed as if she didn't know

which way to go. Forward into the touch at her clit, or back onto the finger working its way into her ass.

"Uhn."

"That's a girl."

TJ saw Jon coat his fingers again with the lube and then he pressed into her a second time. He must have used two fingers this time because Chris hissed and shot forward. TJ took advantage of the exceptional placement of her breasts and sucked a nipple into his mouth.

"Son of a... Oh God. Please," she begged.

When she settled, he released her nipple with a pop. "Payback's a bitch," she growled.

TJ grinned. "Is that a threat or a promise?"

"Teej, I can't wait anymore." Jon withdrew and grabbed hold of her hips.

"Me either." TJ guided his cock to her slick opening. "Come down on me, Chris."

She whimpered as she slowly impaled herself on his straining cock, her inner muscles gripping him until his eyes crossed.

Jon's hips pressed forward.

TJ expected her to balk or put a stop to their double penetration. Sweat beaded Jon's forehead and chest as he worked his cock into her ass.

What he didn't expect was for her to throw her head back and shout, "Keep going. Keep going."

TJ felt Jon's erection creeping along his with only the thin barrier of tissue separating them. When Jon was seated fully, TJ withdrew. Chris sucked in a deep breath and practically followed his cock, which in turn pulled her off Jon.

"Stay still." TJ gripped her hips and slammed into her. He

and Jon set up a rhythm, penetrating and withdrawing, sliding into her body like they'd done this a thousand times. She was perfect. Perfect for both of them and they wouldn't let her go. Somehow they had to make her see.

None of them lasted more than a few minutes.

"I need to...I...please let me..." she cried.

"Yeah, baby. Come for us," TJ broke in. He reached between them and pressed on her exposed clit. Her body seized and she screamed. TJ yanked her hips down and Jon thrust in. Both of them pumped into her at the same time, spurting their come deep inside her body.

Chris collapsed, sprawling her body over TJ's. Jon withdrew from her body and rolled to their side, one hand still on her back, stroking and caressing her as all their breathing slowed.

Finally TJ pulled from her sheath and twisted until she was lying between him and Jon. He flipped a lock of hair from her face. Her eyes drooped but a smile graced her lips, and he kissed the tip of her nose.

"Sleep, baby. I think we could all use a nap." TJ yawned and snuggled closer to the woman he loved.

Chapter Seven

Chris tapped her foot impatiently. TJ and Jon were in Kyle's office, not fifteen feet away and it was too far.

"Shit." As if the last three days spent lazing in their bed hadn't been enough. Only thirty minutes had passed since they'd left her at her desk before their meeting. Not quite lunchtime yet but already this morning she hadn't been able to pull herself from their presence for more than five minutes.

What the hell was happening to her?

Love.

The word slammed into her like a baseball bat to the forehead.

Friday night and the bar seemed like a lifetime away. Her one-night fling had turned into more of a five-nighter and she couldn't see it ending anytime soon.

Didn't want to see it ending.

The thought should have scared her to death. So why did she want so badly to always be a part of them? Why did the mere thought of them being with another woman make her want to throw up?

"Oh, sweetie, how are you?" Aislinn's voice pierced her vision like a needle in a balloon, popping the image of TJ and Jon pleasuring some bimbo.

Aislinn came around the desk and wrapped her arms around Chris's body. "Kyle told me what happened. I'm so sorry."

"Thank you."

"Are you okay? You guys were gone before I knew about it. I should have been there for you."

Chris nodded. "I know you would have." She squeezed her best friend back. "It all happened so fast and I didn't think about calling anyone. TJ and Jon kind of took over and swept us all away. I'll be okay." She took a deep breath. "I think, in the back of my mind, I always knew it would happen this way. I'm kind of surprised it didn't happen sooner." Her throat closed up and tears threatened again. She still couldn't shake the image of her mother lying at the foot of the stairs and she was more than relieved she hadn't actually seen it.

"So he was arrested. He confessed and everything?"

"In a manner of speaking."

"And what about your brother?"

Chris picked up a pen from her desk and twirled it between her finger and thumb. "I don't know. I never heard from him after we left the police station. Last I saw he was spouting something about suing everyone within hearing distance. It was enough to make me leave and never look back."

Aislinn had a sympathetic look on her face. She patted Chris's hand in understanding then a grin curved her lips.

"Lunch at Miguel's? You need a good bowl of tortilla soup."

"Absolutely." This was exactly what she needed. A return to normalcy and lunch with her best friend at the café around the corner where they ate almost every day.

"Great. Let's go early." Aislinn practically bounced.

Chris eyeballed the closed door to Kyle's office. Aislinn

turned to follow her gaze. Her smile grew bigger than ever. "I'm taking it the fling went very well."

"More than you'll ever know," Chris muttered, standing to grab her purse. Thank God she wasn't as tender between her legs anymore. The first couple of days had been a little awkward. Her walking bow-legged, when they'd let her up long enough to walk, must have been amusing.

"Oh my God, girl. I am so getting all the juicy details at lunch."

Christina snorted just as the office door opened. Jon poked his head out. "Where are you ladies headed off to?"

"Lunch," they answered together and giggled as they walked away. Chris's heart pounded. It actually felt strange to leave their presence. Like a string was pulling her back, urging her not to go far. Aislinn looped her hand around Chris's elbow.

"Be careful," Jon growled.

"Oh Lord," Aislinn sighed dramatically. "How did we both get saddled with overprotective brutes?"

"I don't know." *But I'm not inclined to find out how to get unsaddled.*

Ten minutes later they were sitting at their usual outdoor table and gave the waiter, Manuel, their order. Chris lifted her face to the sun, letting it warm her. The past several days had been such a blur, she felt like she was in some kind of time warp.

The skin prickled along the back of her neck. She snapped her gaze around.

"So tell me everything and don't leave anything out." Aislinn's words came from a distance.

Chris didn't see anyone in particular but the feeling of unease wouldn't leave.

"I want all the details."

Sweat trickled between her breasts and shoulder blades.

"Are they as good as the rumors say they are? Not that it's any of my business, but what good is being best friends if you can't share? Chris? Hey, Chris."

Their surroundings came slamming back into Chris. The tinkling of dishes, chattering among the other outdoor patrons, birds chirping, a car honking, the breeze lifting her hair. She sucked in a deep breath and shook her head to clear it of the eerie feeling.

"You look like you've seen a ghost. Are you okay?" Aislinn touched Chris's forearm with light fingers.

Chris lifted the glass of ice water and took a long drink. "I'm fine. Just got the feeling I was being watched or something."

Aislinn craned her neck and twisted in her seat. "I don't see anything out of the ordinary."

"Me neither." Chris gave a tight laugh. "Too bad your vision thing doesn't work on command." She was only half joking. It might be kind of nice to see the future.

Well, maybe not so much. One of the visions Aislinn had seen had been of her fiancé being killed. She'd had enough time to warn Kyle though and divert at least some of the disaster, leaving Kyle very much alive.

"It isn't always a blessing."

Chris smiled. "I guess not."

"Spill."

Their meals arrived before Chris could answer. Miguel's tortilla soup was her absolute favorite. Chris broke the fried strips of tortilla down into the bowl, letting them soak up the spicy, cheesy soup filled with bits of chicken, and lifted the spoon to her mouth. The flavors exploded on her tongue. Today was definitely going to be a two-bowl day.

She was just about to tell the waiter she really wanted another bowl when a chill shot down her spine and a shadow fell over her.

"We're done. Let's get out of here, I'm starving." Jon stood and rotated his head on his shoulders, working out some of the tension. They'd had to fire someone for trying to sell the plans of a special security prototype they'd been developing.

The guy hadn't even had an excuse for them. He'd seen green and gone after it. Thank God they'd caught wind of it before he'd done any real damage.

"Me too." TJ stretched his arms to the ceiling.

Kyle joined in. "Yeah. Let's go find the girls and join them. They haven't been gone long."

The three of them looked at one another and grunted, "Miguel's."

"You'd think they'd get tired of that place." TJ led them from Kyle's office and over to the bank of elevators.

"Aislinn says it's something in the tortilla soup," Kyle said, stepping onto the elevator when it opened with a ding. "All I know is that since you guys have been gone, she hasn't gone to Miguel's, and I don't get the same woman back in the office after lunch that I do when Chris is here."

TJ slapped him on the back with a laugh. "You saying you haven't gotten any since we left?"

Kyle snorted. "Hell no. Not saying that at all. I'm saying I don't get it after lunch." He grinned.

Jon's cell phone rang. Still laughing at Kyle he flipped it open and answered. "Winslow."

"Mr. Winslow, this is Deputy Anders...with the Sheri...De...ment."

Jon stuck his finger in his ear as the door slid shut. Reception would suck in the elevator. "Deputy Anderson?" he repeated. A sense of foreboding shot through him.

"Yes... ...rshall disappeared... Wanted to war...to kee...Ms. Marsh...afe."

"What? I'm in an elevator. You're breaking up." He looked at the phone and cursed when it flashed *no signal* before slamming the lid closed.

"What's going on?" TJ asked, concerned.

"I don't know. It was Deputy Anderson, but it kept cutting out." Jon looked at TJ, conveying the dread starting to settle in the pit of his stomach. "Marshall's gone." And if he was missing then no one would be remiss in thinking he might be headed here. For his daughter. Not after the things he'd spouted after being arrested.

"He's on his way here." There was no doubt in Jon's mind Robert would come after Chris, wanting revenge for having gotten him arrested.

"Fuck." TJ punched the wall.

"That son of bitch wants another piece of Christina." Jon shifted his weight, his body preparing for battle. Everything in him shouted to get to his woman. Now.

"What if they didn't go to Miguel's?" TJ attacked the lobby key with his thumb as if willing the steel trap of a box holding them prisoner to move faster.

"They go to Miguel's every day, you think they'd choose to go somewhere else today? No way," Kyle growled. "It's five minutes on foot which is quicker than getting the car. Besides, if the deputy is just calling you now, chances are he hasn't had enough time to get here yet."

Sure. He might not have had time but what if he did? What if he was already in town and looking for Chris? Damn it! He didn't want to play the what-if game.

The elevator took an eternity to get down to the lobby and an even longer time opening its doors. Jon shoved his way through when the space was barely six inches wide and barreled into the group of people waiting to go up.

He hastily steadied the woman he ran into and mumbled his apologies without missing a beat. TJ slammed through the double plate-glass doors at the same time Jon did with Kyle right on their heels. Miguel's was just a few blocks away. Kyle was right, it would take them longer to get the car than to walk.

Jon forced himself to a fast walk when he wanted to sprint and see for himself Chris was all right. She had to be. He would accept no less. He needed her. *They* needed her in their lives, in their hearts, in their bed. Her and her damn beast of a family-jewels-siccing dog, Clodhopper.

"She's fine." TJ's tone lacked confidence. He lengthened his stride in his eagerness to get to her too.

"Is that why you're running?" Kyle kept pace with them. After all, as Chris's best friend, his woman would be in Roberts's path too, had the man actually shown his face.

They rounded the corner just as a loud crash erupted about thirty feet ahead of them. Seven or eight people jumped back from the short black iron fence surrounding the outdoor portion of the café. Jon's heart thudded and stopped momentarily.

A table flew up and over, toppling dishes and throwing silverware in an arc into the air. A woman screamed, a dog barked, a baby cried.

"Call the police," a man shouted.

Jon took off running, his buddies close behind. He vaulted the three foot tall fence without blinking and took in the scene. What they found surprised them. Robert hadn't come after his daughter.

Carter had come after his sister.

"What are you doing, Carter?" Chris's obscenely calm voice echoed in his head.

"Christ. He's got a gun, Jon. Right hip," TJ said softly and headed to the left.

Jon nodded. "Yep." They kept their voices low so they didn't alert Carter to their presence and reverted to hand signals ingrained from their years in the Special Forces. Kyle's feet made no sound as he moved off to the right.

"You killed her, you fucking bitch." Carter launched himself at her, his hands raised, ready to go for her throat. Chris stood still, looking completely bored, and Jon feared she wouldn't be able to get out of the way in time.

She didn't have to. Aislinn's foot shot out, sending Carter sprawling to the concrete in a drunken mess. He spluttered and screeched, crawling to his hands and knees, stunned.

Chris picked her way between a fallen chair and bits of glass and ceramic to stand in front of the man her brother had become, and Jon breathed a sigh of relief. Christina Marshall wasn't a woman to be treated with kid gloves. Not that he'd ever thought she needed to be, but still.

"I wasn't even there," she hissed. Jon, TJ and Kyle edged closer. She glanced up and directly into Jon's eyes. Hers widened, and Jon gave a quick shake of his head and covered his lips with a finger to keep her from giving them away. He watched her gaze flick to Kyle and TJ. She knew she wasn't alone. Aislinn saw them too if the look on her face was any indication.

"That's right, you bitch," Carter snarled.

Jon saw the miniscule flinch and the narrowing of Christina's lips and eyes and could have groaned.

"If you had been, she wouldn't have fought with me day and night. She wouldn't have alienated her son and I wouldn't have had to kill her."

Jon was less than four feet away, separated by the overturned table, but he saw the way Chris's face blanched and heard her sharp intake of breath. Robert Marshall hadn't killed his wife. Her own son had. Because he'd felt ignored.

Kyle and TJ flanked Jon but stayed back so they wouldn't be seen. No one wanted to give Carter a reason to draw his gun and possibly get a shot off in the middle of the crowded café. A couple of men scooted closer, trying to be heroes no doubt. TJ warned them off in some silent way Jon didn't see with his focus on Carter.

"She never fought you, you bastard. She took our father's meaty fists against her face and body every night and forgave him every morning. She protected us both from his hands and if she had left like I did, she would still be alive. *You* killed her because of some deflated ego." The crowd gasped at her revelation while sirens sounded in the distance.

Christ, he would tan her sweet little ass later for taunting her brother like this. TJ and he would take immeasurable pleasure in doing so too. Despite the situation, Jon felt his cock harden as he envisioned her cheeks pinkened by his hand and how wet her pussy would be by the time he sank deep inside her.

Carter gave a guttural cry and reached for the gun.

It barely cleared the waistband of his filthy jeans before TJ, Jon and Kyle were on him. Jon didn't even remember leaping over the table blocking his way. He saw metal and something in him snapped.

He gripped Carter's wrist and slammed it against the ground. An agonized cry erupted from the other man. The gun clattered across the concrete, safely away.

The takedown was almost too easy. Perhaps because Carter was drunk and off his full faculties. A police car squealed to a halt on the street behind them and the crowd started in on what they'd seen.

Jon kept his knee planted squarely in the small of Carter's back.

"Get off me," he shrieked, tossing and turning and trying to shake Jon loose.

"You okay, baby?" TJ wrapped Chris in a bear hug. Jon signaled one of the officers over. He needed to be in on the touching TJ was receiving, not here bent over the raving lunatic who'd threatened his woman.

Chris nodded, a snarl curling her lip with distaste as she looked down at her brother currently being handcuffed.

"We had a bit of a warning, so neither of us got hurt."

TJ, Kyle and Jon turned to Aislinn, expecting her to have had a vision. Aislinn shook her head.

"Nope, wasn't me." She pointed at Chris and all eyes turned to her.

"What?" she asked innocently.

TJ grasped her hands. "Sweetheart. Is there something you need to tell us?"

Her face scrunched up. "No. No! Good Lord, I got this tingly feeling on the back of my neck and then there was this shadow over us. It could have been the way he very loudly called me the trashy whore who killed her mother in front of the entire café. Caused enough of a commotion for Aislinn and me to get up, which is when he shoved the table over."

Aislinn snorted. "Oh and that had nothing to do with you calling him a drunken pig who needed to go wallow in his miserable life somewhere else."

Jon leaned in and whispered in Chris's ear, letting his hand wander to her ass. "You will pay for antagonizing the man trying to kill you, sweetheart."

Carter fought the police, jerking against their hold. It took three of them to subdue him and finally drag him to the squad car, kicking and spitting his profanities and accusations all the way.

"I wasn't antagonizing him. He called me a killing whore. Was I not supposed to defend myself? I can't believe it was him all along. I never thought... I... Do you think the cops will keep him or let him go?"

TJ took her elbow and started guiding her back to the Turner Industries building. "They won't have a choice since you're going to press charges for assault."

"Will it stick? He didn't touch me."

"No, but the table did." Aislinn pointed to Chris's hip. "Remember, he flipped it up and it bounced off you."

"Son of a bitch, Chris." TJ jerked to a stop and started pulling her shirt from her pants so he could see if there were marks. Jon assisted. "Where did he get you? Are you hurt bad?"

Chris pushed at their hands. "Um, hello, public sidewalk here. Get your hands out of my pants."

Jon grinned. "Then we'd better get home, because I want nothing other than to have my hands in your pants."

"I see Sergeant Watts over there. I'll tell him we'll bring her in later. I'm sure they've got questions."

"Who's Sergeant Watts?" Chris asked as Jon tried to pull

her away.

"A friend of ours," Jon answered and then called over his shoulder to Kyle while he propelled Chris down the street. "We're taking the rest of the day off."

"Bye," Jon heard Aislinn yell behind them, her voice amused.

"Are we even going to make it home?" Chris grunted. "Good Lord, slow down."

Jon pushed the pace and somehow he and TJ made Chris keep up. No way would he slow down. Witnessing her brother trying to take her out of his life had been too much. He needed to reconnect with her. To do that he needed to get as close to her as humanly possible—inside her. Buried deep where she wouldn't know where one of them ended and the other began. Either of them because Jon needed TJ there with them as well.

If TJ was in the same shape as Jon, they might not make it home, but she was right, they didn't need to get arrested for public indecency.

"We'll make it home." He eyeballed the remaining distance between them and his car parked in the lot next to Turner Industries. "We have to for what I have in store for you," Jon growled.

Chapter Eight

The front door closed behind them with a definitive thud, adding to the growing thump her heart was currently beating. TJ had driven this time while Jon kept her occupied in the backseat. Distracted, more like. There wasn't any part of her body his hands and mouth hadn't touched. He'd been especially tender at her hip where an ugly bruise had already shown itself.

Her nipples were rock hard, her clit throbbed and she was breathless. Jon had her primed and ready with all his backseat foreplay. She rounded on him, grabbing his shirt and hauling him to her.

"Where were we?" She ignored his look of surprise and attacked his lips.

TJ sandwiched her between them, nestling his thick cock against her ass, promising wickedness. His hands came up, dragging her shirt with them then palming her breasts Jon had so thoughtfully freed from their confinement in the car.

A second later, Jon flicked open the button at her waist. She heard the rasp of the zipper over her moans as TJ pinched and rolled her nipples into even harder points.

She needed them. Needed both to fill her mind with something other than the ugliness her brother had brought.

Her pants were pushed down gently over her sore hip. As soon as they reached her knees, all tenderness was gone. Jon's booted foot stepped on the crotch and shoved them to the floor. TJ knelt and helped her step out all while his tongue roamed her backside. His hands kneaded her flesh, spreading her cheeks so his tongue could rim her.

She squirmed at the strange feeling, thinking she should be disgusted but not managing to summon anything but pleasure. Oh God, they were turning her into a depraved wanton. TJ's fingers tapped her inner thighs.

"Spread your legs, baby."

She did, sucking in a breath when two lean fingers speared into her core.

"You're wet, Chris."

Well, duh. She swallowed and laid her head on Jon's chest. He rubbed her back and held her still for the fingered assault on her pussy and the tonguing of her tiny opening farther back.

After stripping her shirt off, Jon added his fingers between her legs, rubbing a slow circle around her exposed clit.

"Shit." She bit her lip and her knees sagged. After these last few days they were experts at playing her body.

"Uh-uh, sugar. Not yet. We have a little business to attend to first."

"What?" She came out of her stupor to see a gleam in Jon's eye. What the hell?

TJ's clothes brushed up her naked skin, chilling her. He nibbled on her ear. "What were you thinking taunting Carter like that?" His hands slid up her sides to return to her nipples, giving them a tug and nearly causing her to sink to the floor.

She shook her head. "What did you want me to do, cower?"

"Yes," they both said emphatically.

Jon sighed. "We want you to be safe, not put yourself in the direct line of fire. Didn't you see the gun?"

"No, I was too busy dodging the flying iron table and chairs and dishes. And then he pissed me off by calling me a whore."

TJ turned her face to his with his thumb under her chin. "You are not a whore." His mouth wandered from her lips, over to her ear, down her jaw to the crook of her shoulder and neck. Chris tilted her head to give him better access. "All the same, you need to be spanked."

"For what?" she breathed, not really caring when Jon's lips surrounded one of her nipples and tugged it into his mouth.

Somehow they managed to move across the floor, all while tangled together, kisses still being applied. When they reached the couch, Chris was turned so her belly rested along the back. TJ stalked around to the front and climbed onto the cushions on his knees, his gaze never leaving hers. His fingers went to the buttons of his fly. Chris dropped her stare to watch each button push through its hole in slow motion.

His cock—long, thick and looking painfully hard—thrust out when he pulled it from his boxers. She licked her lips.

"Yeah, baby, get those lips wet." TJ fisted his erection and stroked it from base to tip.

A hand in the middle of her back bent her over the couch so her head hung above the chaise part of the three-part monstrosity. His calloused hands smoothed over her buttocks and hips, paying special attention to the humongous bruise blooming to life.

"Does this hurt, sugar?"

She gulped. "No." She had a feeling her ass was going to burn like hell in a minute and cover up any hurt she might feel anyway. So why wasn't she protesting and running screaming from their house?

Jon chuckled. When she felt him next, he was naked. His cock prodded her slick entrance when he parted her thighs. It felt so good. She caught herself with her hands on the couch to keep from falling headfirst. And still, TJ's hand worked his length. He moved closer, first kneeling on the chaise, then working his legs out in front of him so he was spread eagle, one leg draped over either side of the chaise. He helped her balance herself by putting her hands next to his thighs. His penis saluted her not five inches from her face, its head shiny with pre-come.

Now she knew why they'd chosen this position.

A sharp slap resonated in the otherwise silent room a split second before the pain radiated through her bottom.

"Fuck. I wasn't ready," she cried, looking over her shoulder at the deviant grinning behind her.

"And your point is?" Jon caressed the heat blossoming over her left butt cheek, taking some of the sting away.

"Suck me, Chris." TJ's hands guided her head back to his cock. It was just far enough out of reach she had to stand on her tiptoes to get close. She squealed as Jon lifted her off her feet, but it got the job done. Her lips brushed the tip of TJ's cock and he sucked in a breath.

"Perfect," Jon murmured, running a hand up and down her spine.

"Take me in your mouth," TJ practically snarled.

"Be patient, would you?" She glared up at him. *Smack.* "Yowch!"

"See? You're back to the taunting again. That's why you're in this position in the first place." Jon smacked his hand down again.

Chris squeezed her eyes closed as the burn settled and turned into something else, leaving her clit begging to be touched and her pussy sopping wet.

"You mean it has nothing to do with the fact you're in perfect alignment?" She wiggled on his cock, teasing the swollen folds between her legs, and received another slap on her rear.

"Suck," TJ commanded in a gravelly voice meant to shock her. He'd propped himself up with his hands behind him on the chaise. If anything, the man was being tortured by having her mouth so close yet so far away.

She took pity and wrapped her lips around the fat head, licking off the salty essence of him. She heard his groan and imagined him dropping his head back in ecstasy.

Chris took delight in sucking him in as deep as she could before gagging around his circumference. The whole blow job thing was getting easier, more palatable. She wasn't sure she was ready to swallow yet, but she was getting closer to the idea of trying it maybe. Maybe.

Jon pressed forward, lodging the head of his cock inside her opening. She moaned, inadvertently taking TJ deeper than she ever had before, and he moaned too.

Another slap on her rump had her rearing up, arching her back and dragging up on TJ's cock. His hand tangled in her hair, bringing her back down. She swirled her tongue along the thick vein running the length of his penis and flicked at the sensitive spot under the head.

Jon thrust in, impaling her with every inch of his cock and slapping her again. The tingling sensation wound its way through her torso, aiming for her clit. If he would just touch her, she would explode.

Up and down, she worked TJ, leaning her weight on one hand so she could play with his balls. It worked for a minute then she had to give up before her elbow gave out. She went back to bobbing her head. TJ was too far gone to care.

"I'm gonna come," he warned.

Could she take it? Jon pounded into her and somehow found her clit with his fingers, pinching the taut little bundle of nerves. Colors swirled.

"Chris," TJ barked.

She couldn't think, not with the way Jon played her vagina. Certainly not when his wet thumb found the tight ring of muscle in the back and pushed in, adding to what was already happening down there and the orgasm hovering just out of reach.

TJ's hand gripped her hair and pulled. Chris sucked him back in. His hips shot upward, shoving his cock to the back of her throat. He came with a growl, his cock jerking in her mouth, the thick cream splashing down her throat. She either swallowed or choked.

It wasn't bad. Not really what she'd thought it would be like. Warm and salty but she suspected he was far enough back she didn't get the full taste of him. TJ collapsed into the chaise, breathing hard and patting her hair.

Jon grunted behind her, each thrust keeping her moving on TJ's softening penis and making his abs spasm with each pass. She lapped at him, licking him clean.

Jon pulled his thumb from her anus. The action caused her to squeeze his cock with her pussy.

"Yes," he cried. One hard hand grasped her unbruised hip, pulling her back as he pounded forward. His fingers pressed on her clit and an intense orgasm washed over her. She lifted her head from TJ and fought back a scream.

Jon slammed home one last time and held himself rigid while he emptied his come into her core.

Chris flopped down, no longer able to hold herself up. Her forehead rested against TJ's cock. She inhaled his scent with every harsh breath and felt it grow.

They were going to kill her.

"Come here, baby." TJ tugged her over the back of the couch with his hands under her arms so she sprawled over his body.

"Hey," Jon complained as his cock slipped from deep inside her. Chris couldn't help but giggle. She tucked her nose into the crease of TJ's neck and shoulder and sighed.

"I love you," she whispered. Her eyes widened and she held her breath. She hadn't meant to say the words out loud.

Jon vaulted the couch to sit beside them. His hand landed on her thigh, near the bruise, and caressed lightly.

"Good thing. We wouldn't want to have to keep you here against your will."

She heard the smile in Jon's voice. Her heart thudded. Keep her here? Could she do that? Could she put all her trust in two men after everything she'd witnessed with her father?

Who the hell was she kidding? She'd already given them her trust the minute she'd let them blindfold her.

TJ lifted her chin and kissed her with a tender mouth. "We love you too. Stay with us. Be a part of us."

Jon's lips traveled up her spine. He knelt on the floor and leaned over to look in her eyes. "Yes. Stay. Let us love you forever."

The waterworks started. She sniffed and buried her nose. Jon pushed the long hair from her face and kissed her cheek.

"Don't cry, sugar. It's a simple yes or no answer."

"Yes. Yes." She rolled to her back and let the two men enfold her in their arms. She didn't know how it would work out and she didn't care. She only knew she couldn't stand the thought of not being here with them.

An angry bark erupted from down the hall.

"Oops," TJ said sheepishly.

Chris brushed them both off and sat forward. She crossed her arms over her chest and fought a smile.

"You shut Clodhopper in the bathroom again?"

About the Author

Between being a wife, mommy, cleaning woman, chauffeur, coach and leader, there are a few minutes left to sneak in some writing time. Annmarie McKenna loves to hear from readers. You can visit her website at www.annmariemckenna.com or her blog at www.annmariemckenna.blogspot.com. Send an email to annmarmck@yahoo.com.

Welcome to Fantasm Island! Leave your inhibitions at the door and let your fantasies soar

Fantasmagorical

© 2007 Annmarie McKenna

That's what the brochure said anyway. A week long fling with a stranger. Where's the harm in that? Take a compatibility quiz and a slew of other health tests, sign a strict privacy agreement and give license to any sexual fantasy you've ever had. Evan Knight couldn't wait.

Gabe and Lance have been searching for their perfect third for what seems like forever. One look at the woman he and his best friend and lover Lance have chosen to claim during her time on the island, and Gabe thinks they may have finally found her.

But what if Evan isn't interested in more than the fling she signed up for? Or worse, what if she can't handle two men who are into each other too? Gabe and Lance have one week to convince Evan that the three of them belong together...and they'll use every bit of seduction in their arsenal to make sure when the fantasy ends, their reality together will only just be beginning.

Warning, this title contains the following: explicit fantasmagorical sex, graphic language, ménage a trois, and hot nekkid man-love.

Enjoy the following excerpt from Fantasmagorical...

Gabe Lariet had recognized her as his the second she'd walked in the door. Her long, dark brown hair was caught up in a haphazard ponytail that had worked itself loose in the oppressive heat of Fantasm Island. He itched to rip the offending elastic off so he could see the thick strands flow over his thighs and belly when she sucked him off.

Or better yet, over Lance's cock while Gabe buried himself in her pussy. A pussy he knew by the tremble of her body and the scent of her essence was already wet and preparing itself for them.

He pressed his erection into the small of her back and she melted into him. She was tiny compared to him. More than a head shorter. They would need to be careful not to hurt her the first time they took her together. And make no mistake, they would most definitely fuck her at the same time. They'd shared women many, many times over their long friendship, especially since discovering some time a few years back that what would make them whole would be a third. A woman to complete their circle.

He plucked at the woman's distended nipples through the thin cotton of her shirt as she watched her friend take a good amount of Zach's length down her throat. It looked like the friend could do some major sucking but she didn't do anything for him. His taste ran to a certain petite brunette who would fall to the floor if he took a step back right now.

Gabe supported her with his arm across her smooth tummy and continued to palm her breasts with the other. They were small, but damn if her nipples weren't hard as rocks.

"I'm claiming you," he growled in her ear, glancing around

at her face in time to see her eyes slide shut. She pursed her lips and nodded acceptance.

There weren't always matches at Fantasmagorical. He'd never had it happen to him, but occasionally it did happen that a guest wasn't claimed for the entire week. In those cases, the guest's name was put into a pool and they were then paired by the day. They spent their week being doted on by several different employees who'd been hired for the sole purpose of keeping unclaimed guests happy.

Gabe and Lance, on the other hand, had made lots of women happy. Women looking for a ménage or a break from their traditional bedroom antics. They'd even had several return customers to the island who'd asked for them specifically, but they'd yet to connect with one on a spiritual level. The day would come eventually, either here on the island or back at home in Florida. And when they found her, they'd keep her forever.

Fantasm Island, owned by his own eccentric billionaire uncle, got its business through word of mouth. Usually women, sometimes men, came to the resort ready for intense sexual freedom. Anything goes. Guests were tested both physically and mentally and only those who passed with flying colors were invited to come.

"I'm claiming you too." Lance's voice rumbled beside him. The woman jumped in his arms and twisted to see who'd spoken. Her eyes widened to quarter-sized disks and she gasped. She looked around him at the group of women pouting after Lance.

"You're ours," Gabe said and tugged her toward the rear exit. "Get her bag," he threw over his shoulder.

"Already taken care of."

"But my—"

"Your friend is being well taken care of too, by Zach. Believe me." Gabe took one elbow, Lance the other and headed to their quarters. If he didn't relieve the tension in his cock soon, it was liable to explode before he got inside her.

Palm trees lined all the pathways coming to and from the main resort building. Parties, dinners and dances were held at the big building. Smaller huts housed specialty rooms for any fantasy a guest could think up. If they couldn't find what they wanted, the situation could be created.

"I can't wait, Gabe." Lance drew to a stop along the balustrade outside.

She squeaked when he backed her up to the concrete ledge and trapped her between his hands, which he rested beside her.

"You are beautiful." He nuzzled her throat. "What's your name?"

She gave a hysterical little laugh and tilted her head back to give Lance better access. Gabe moved to the other side and added his mouth.

"This is really weird." She moaned.

"But what you want, right?" Gabe whispered, licking along the vein.

When she paused too long, Lance said, "Answer him, sweetheart."

"Yes." The word hissed from deep in her lungs.

"From now on you answer us the first time." Gabe placed a hand at her waist and slid it beneath her shirt. Lance's met his at her breasts so they each held one. They manipulated the hardened tips simultaneously.

She made a disparaging sound but didn't balk at their command. It was part of her profile. She wished to be a submissive in every way that mattered sexually. Of course, her profile only provided a photo, not a name. All the “employees” were given profiles for each guest. It allowed them to claim the guest that interested them the most the minute they walked in the door.

They weren’t given a name in case the guest desired to stay somewhat anonymous. If things didn’t work out, both guest and employee were allowed to trade at a mixer later in the week, or, if things were really bad right from the start, the owner would see to it the guest was directed to another employee. He wanted everyone to be happy.

“This one time will be your only warning. From here on out you will be punished. Do you understand?” Lance demanded.

Printed in the United States
118629LV00012B/172-174/P

9 781599 988054